The
PUFFIN
TREASURY
— of —
CHILDREN'S
STORIES

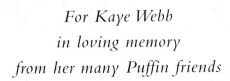

For Kaye Webb
in loving memory
from her many Puffin friends

VIKING/PUFFIN

Published by the Penguin Group
Penguin Books Ltd, 27 Wrights Lane, London W8 5TZ, England
Penguin Books USA Inc., 375 Hudson Street, New York, New York 10014, USA
Penguin Books Australia Ltd, Ringwood, Victoria, Australia
Penguin Books Canada Ltd, 10 Alcorn Avenue, Toronto, Ontario, Canada M4V 3B2
Penguin Books (NZ) Ltd, 182-190 Wairau Road, Auckland 10, New Zealand
Penguin Books Ltd, Registered Offices: Harmondsworth, Middlesex, England
First published 1996
1 3 5 7 9 10 8 6 4 2
This edition copyright © Penguin Books Ltd, 1996
The acknowledgements on pp. 309-310 constitute an extension of this copyright page;
illustrations not listed remain the copyright © of the individual illustrators credited, 1996
Stories selected and introduced by Anna Trenter
The moral rights of the authors and illustrators have been asserted
All rights reserved. Without limiting the rights under copyright reserved above, no part of
this publication may be reproduced, stored in or introduced into a retrieval system, or transmitted,
in any form or by any means (electronic, mechanical, photocopying, recording or otherwise), without
the prior written permission of both the copyright owner and the above publisher of this book
Made and printed in Italy by de Agostini
A CIP catalogue record for this book is available from the British Library
ISBN 0–670–87009–9

The PUFFIN TREASURY of CHILDREN'S STORIES

PUFFIN BOOKS

CONTENTS

∾

FOREWORD

∽

'ONE of the special charms of books is that they can give you so many different kinds of pleasure. Some will increase your knowledge of the world in general (as well as telling a cracking good story), some introduce you to fantastic places and characters which set your imaginations whirling. Others are reassuring and comfortable; showing you everyday people coping with the kind of difficulties you can imagine happening to you. But the very best thing is that you can enjoy them anywhere, at any time – they become your private world which no one can invade or disturb.'

These words were written some years ago by Kaye Webb, the inspired Editor of Puffin Books who introduced children to an astonishing wealth of stories, and who remained 'Queen Puffin' for many readers until her death in January 1996.

Kaye's words are as true now as they were when she wrote them. Books are still the doorway to wonderful new worlds. A reader can have thrilling adventures that seem as real as if they had actually happened. Time travel becomes possible; animals talk; people from fairy tales come alive, and legendary kings regain their thrones. The gap between fantasy and reality is small. Books can close the gap for a while and welcome the reader to another world.

The stories and extracts in this anthology offer something to every reader. Some, such as *Winnie-the-Pooh* and *The Happy Prince* have been favourites for many years. Others, like *The Worst Witch* and *Mr Majeika* have been discovered and loved much more recently. One thing is certain, whether you prefer to follow Lucy and Edmund into Narnia in *The Lion, The Witch and the Wardrobe*, or meet the tin man in *The Wizard of Oz*, or steal a dragon's treasure in *The Hobbit*, or even face Marley's ghost in *A Christmas Carol*, there are stories and pictures to suit every taste and mood.

Books are for everyone, and the pleasure they give lasts a lifetime. When you dip into this Treasury, you will find out why.

Beatrix Potter

THE TALE OF PETER RABBIT

ILLUSTRATED BY THE AUTHOR

ONCE upon a time there were four little Rabbits, and their names were – Flopsy, Mopsy, Cotton-tail, and Peter. They lived with their Mother in a sand-bank, underneath the root of a very big fir-tree.

'Now, my dears,' said old Mrs Rabbit one morning, 'you may go into the fields or down the lane, but don't go into Mr McGregor's garden: your Father had an accident there; he was put in a pie by Mrs McGregor.

'Now run along, and don't get into mischief. I am going out.'

Then old Mrs Rabbit took a basket and her umbrella, and went through the wood to the baker's. She bought a loaf of brown bread and five currant buns.

Flopsy, Mopsy, and Cotton-tail, who were good little bunnies, went down

the lane to gather blackberries.

But Peter, who was very naughty, ran straight away to Mr McGregor's garden, and squeezed under the gate!

First he ate some lettuces and some French beans; and then he ate some radishes.

And then, feeling rather sick, he went to look for some parsley.

But round the end of a cucumber frame, whom should he meet but Mr McGregor!

Mr McGregor was on his hands and knees planting out young cabbages, but he jumped up and ran after Peter, waving a rake and calling out, 'Stop thief!'

Peter was most dreadfully frightened; he rushed all over the garden, for he had forgotten the way back to the gate.

He lost one of his shoes among the cabbages, and the other shoe amongst the potatoes.

After losing them, he ran on four legs and went faster, so that I think he might have got away altogether if he had not unfortunately run into a gooseberry net, and got caught by the large buttons on his jacket. It was a blue jacket with brass buttons, quite new.

Peter gave himself up for lost, and shed big tears; but his sobs were overheard by some friendly sparrows, who flew to him in great excitement, and implored him to exert himself.

Mr McGregor came up with a sieve, which he intended to pop upon the top of Peter; but Peter wriggled out just in time, leaving his jacket behind him.

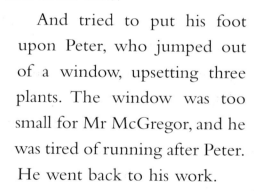

And rushed into the tool-shed, and jumped into a can. It would have been a beautiful thing to hide in, if it had not had so much water in it.

Mr McGregor was quite sure that Peter was somewhere in the tool-shed, perhaps hidden underneath a flower-pot. He began to turn them over carefully, looking under each.

Presently Peter sneezed – 'Kertyschoo!' Mr McGregor was after him in no time.

And tried to put his foot upon Peter, who jumped out of a window, upsetting three plants. The window was too small for Mr McGregor, and he was tired of running after Peter. He went back to his work.

Peter sat down to rest; he was out of breath and trembling with fright, and he had not the least idea which way to go. Also he was very damp with sitting in that can.

After a time he began to wander about, going lippity – lippity – not very fast, and looking all round.

He found a door in a wall; but it was locked, and there was no room for a fat little rabbit to squeeze underneath.

An old mouse was running in and out over the stone door-step, carrying peas and beans to her family in the wood. Peter asked her the way to the gate, but she had such a large pea in her mouth that she could not answer. She only shook her head at him. Peter began to cry.

Then he tried to find his way straight across the garden, but he became more and more puzzled. Presently, he came to a pond where Mr McGregor filled his water-cans. A white cat was staring at some gold-fish, she sat very, very still, but now and then the tip of her tail twitched as if it were alive. Peter thought it best to go away without speaking to her; he had heard about cats from his cousin, little Benjamin Bunny.

He went back towards the tool-shed, but suddenly, quite close to him, he heard the noise of a hoe – scr-r-ritch, scratch, scratch, scritch. Peter scuttered underneath the bushes. But presently, as nothing happened, he came out, and climbed upon a wheelbarrow and peeped over. The first thing he saw was Mr McGregor hoeing onions. His back was turned towards Peter, and beyond him was the gate!

Peter got down very quietly off the wheelbarrow, and started running as fast as he could go, along a straight walk behind some black-currant bushes.

Mr McGregor caught sight of him at the corner, but Peter did not care. He slipped underneath the gate, and was safe at last in the wood outside the garden.

Mr McGregor hung up the little jacket and the shoes for a scarecrow to frighten the blackbirds.

Peter never stopped running or looked behind him till he got home to the big fir-tree.

He was so tired that he flopped down upon the nice soft sand on the floor of the rabbit-hole and shut his eyes. His mother was busy cooking; she wondered what he had done with his clothes. It was the second little jacket and pair of shoes that Peter had lost in a fortnight!

I am sorry to say that Peter was not very well during the evening.

His mother put him to bed, and made some camomile tea; and she gave a dose of it to Peter!

'One table-spoonful to be taken at bed-time.'

But Flopsy, Mopsy, and Cotton-tail had bread and milk and blackberries for supper.

Hans Christian Andersen

THE EMPEROR'S NEW CLOTHES

RETOLD BY WENDY COOLING
ILLUSTRATED BY IAN BECK

ONCE upon a time in a distant land there lived an Emperor who was known the world over for his extraordinary love of fine clothes. All his riches were used to buy the most beautiful silks, satins, brocades, laces and trimmings, and to pay the cleverest and most creative tailors in the land. He was the leader of fashion.

Unlike other kings and emperors he was not interested in his army, although he did like his soldiers to look splendid when they escorted him on royal visits. He was bored by government and left his ministers to run the country. All the Emperor cared about was showing off his latest outfits and appearing in public looking finer and richer than anyone else. He was always changing his clothes, sometimes a dozen times a day and, although most rulers are to be found in their council chambers, this Emperor was always sure to be in his wardrobe!

In the Emperor's city, life was full of pleasure and many visitors came to enjoy the parties and the theatres — and sometimes to swindle the honest citizens.

One day two clever swindlers arrived in town. They claimed to be weavers and said they could weave the finest cloth imaginable. They claimed that their colours were as delicate as butterflies' wings, their cloth as light as gossamer and their patterns beautiful and unusually intricate. But more than this, they declared that their cloth had a magical quality and was invisible to all who were particularly stupid, or not fit to do the jobs they had been given.

The wild claims of the swindlers soon reached the ears of the Emperor and he was intrigued. 'The cloth would make the most wonderful clothes,' he thought, 'and how splendid it would be to tell the wise from the stupid amongst my people.' The more the Emperor thought about the cloth the more irresistible the claims of the swindlers became and he summoned them to his palace.

'Weave the cloth at once,' commanded the Emperor, already longing to show off to his people a fabric the like of which had never been seen before.

The swindlers asked for their money in advance, then they set up two looms and pretended to begin their work. They ordered golden threads and fine silks which went straight into their bags, and they pretended to weave at their empty looms. They worked day and night, talking to no one.

Soon the Emperor was anxious to know how the weaving was going. Although he was quite confident of his own cleverness and was sure he would be able to see the magic cloth, he felt a little too uneasy to go to the looms himself. Instead he sent his wise old Minister, a man he trusted completely and was very fond of, thinking, 'He's a clever man who does a good job, he will surely see the fabric and report back to me.'

The Minister went rather nervously to inspect the weaving, concerned because by now the whole city had heard of the magic quality of the cloth and everybody was talking about it.

The swindlers invited the Minister into their room saying, 'Don't you love the pattern and the shine of the cloth? Have you ever seen such colours?' But the Minister could see nothing.

The wise old man peered closely at the looms and put out a hand to feel the cloth, but there was nothing there. 'Can it be that I am stupid?' wondered the Minister. 'I have never thought so before, but if I am I must be careful to let no one know – for surely I am not unfit for my job.'

'What is your opinion of the cloth, Minister?' asked one of the swindlers. 'Is it not the most splendid design you have ever seen?'

'Oh yes,' replied the Minister. 'It is truly amazing. The colours are dazzling and the cloth is finer than I would have thought possible. I shall go and tell the Emperor at once how much I admire it.'

The swindlers described the cloth in great detail and the

Minister listened carefully so that he could repeat their words to the Emperor – and that is just what he did.

The swindlers demanded more money, more golden thread and silk, and pretended to work still longer at their looms. But the thread and silk went straight into their pockets and the looms were empty.

Soon the Emperor, impatient to know how the work was going, sent another honest man to check on progress.

'Isn't it looking wonderful?' remarked one of the swindlers as the official came in to inspect the cloth. But the official too could see nothing and, like the Minister before him, dared not admit it. How could he say he had seen only empty looms and still be considered wise?

'I am sure I am good at my job,' he thought. 'I am not stupid, but I can't risk honesty.' And so, like the Minister, he spoke in glowing terms of the wonderful cloth he could not see and the extraordinary designs that did not exist.

Now everyone was talking about the cloth and the whole city was buzzing with excitement. The Emperor could wait no longer and went with some of his courtiers and the Minister and the official who had been before to see the magical cloth for himself.

The swindlers as usual were only pretending to weave, and still their looms were empty. The two men who had visited before quickly pointed out the wonders of the material that they thought perhaps the others could see.

The Emperor looked at the empty looms and was shocked, but he managed to keep his face expressionless. 'I can see nothing!' he thought. 'Can it be that I am stupid? Am I not fit to be Emperor?'

He looked closer and closer and could still see nothing. Soon, like the others before him, he was nodding his head in approval and saying, 'Yes, it is very beautiful. It is unlike anything I have seen before.' How could he admit he could see nothing and be thought a fool?

The courtiers with him, desperate to be thought wise, all praised the cloth although they too could see nothing. They spoke in turn, each more extravagantly than the one before. Cries of 'Amazing!' 'Wonderful!' 'Spectacular!' 'Unbelievable!' 'Superb!' echoed around the chamber.

The Emperor ordered the swindlers to make him some clothes out of the cloth to wear at a great procession due to take place the next week. To show his delight and approval he gave each swindler a medal, the Emperor's Cross, to wear from his buttonhole, and he declared them to be Lords of the Loom.

The swindlers pretended to work all through the night right up

to the day of the procession, burning sixteen candles at the window so that the people of the city could see them. They pretended to take the cloth from the loom, to cut out the invisible garments with a huge pair of scissors and to work away with needles and thread. At last, as the morning of the procession came, they announced, 'The clothes are ready. Let the Emperor know.'

The atmosphere was tense as the Emperor entered the room. The swindlers held the invisible garments against him, asking him to admire the coat, the trousers and the cloak with its long flowing train. They remarked on the lightness of the garments. 'They are so light,' they said, 'it will feel as though you have nothing on at all.'

The confident swindlers smiled at everybody in a relaxed fashion. 'May we now dress Your Majesty in the new clothes?' asked one, and the Emperor slowly took off his clothes.

The swindlers helped him into his new, invisible trousers, jacket and cloak and the Emperor looked into the mirror, still able to see nothing. His servants admired his clothes saying, 'You look wonderful, Your Majesty, the fit is perfect.' But still the Emperor could see nothing.

The Emperor took his place under a plumed canopy and waited for the grand procession to begin. 'Doesn't the suit shimmer in the sunlight,' he commented to his courtiers. In return they mentioned the exquisite fit of the clothes and the lightness of the material.

In the city the people thronged the streets, all of them remarking on the beauty and quality of the Emperor's new clothes. No one wanted to be thought stupid. No one admitted that they could not see the clothes.

The Emperor's procession made its way through the town and seemed to be a huge success until, suddenly, a little child who knew nothing of adult pride, called out, 'The Emperor has nothing on!'

The boy's father said, 'Listen to the voice of an innocent child.'

Whispers spread through the crowd. Voices could be heard saying, 'He has nothing on!' or 'Listen to the child!'. Soon the voices were louder and were crying, 'The Emperor has nothing on!' and the Emperor knew that it was true. He knew he had been fooled. But he was a proud man and although inside he cringed with embarrassment, he held himself straight and walked on with dignity, and his gentlemen-in-waiting walked proudly behind him, holding the lighter than cobweb train that really was not there at all.

Margaret Mahy

THE RUNAWAY REPTILES

ILLUSTRATED BY TONY ROSS

SIR Hamish Hawthorn, the famous old explorer, was not happy.

'Oh, Marilyn,' he cried to his favourite niece. 'I long to go exploring up the Orinoco river once more, but who will look after my pets?'

'The Reverend Crabtree next door will feed the cats, I'm sure,' said Marilyn. 'He is a very kind-hearted man. And I will take care of the alligator for you.'

'But Marilyn,' Sir Hamish said, 'what about your neighbour? He might object to alligators.'

Marilyn lived in Marigold Avenue – a most respectable street. The house next door was exactly the same as hers. It had the same green front door, the same garden and the same marigolds. A man called Archie Lightfoot lived there. He was rather handsome, but being handsome was not everything. Would he enjoy having a twenty-foot Orinoco alligator next door?

'Don't worry, Uncle dear,' said Marilyn. 'I shall work something out.'

At that exact moment, by a curious coincidence, Archie Lightfoot was opening an important-looking letter.

Dear Mr Lightfoot, he read.
Your great-aunt — who died last week — has left you her stamp album, full of rare and valuable stamps.

'Terrific!' shouted Archie. Though he had never met his great-aunt, he had inherited her great love of stamps. Now, it seemed, he had inherited her stamp album as well. He read on eagerly.

There is one condition. You must give a good home to your aunt's twenty-foot Nile crocodile. If you refuse, you don't get the stamp collection. Those are the terms of the will.

'What will Marilyn Hawthorn say?' muttered Archie Lightfoot. 'A beautiful girl like that will not want a twenty-foot Nile crocodile on the lawn next door. I will have to work something out.'

That night, Marilyn Hawthorn tossed and turned. She could not sleep. In the end she decided to get up and make herself some toast. She could see the light next door shining on the marigolds. Archie Lightfoot was evidently having something to eat as well.

There is something about midnight meals that makes people have clever ideas. Sure enough, on the stroke of twelve, Marilyn Hawthorn suddenly thought of the answer to her problem.

The next day she ran up a large blue sun bonnet and a pretty shawl on her sewing machine, and borrowed the biggest motorized wheelchair she could find. Then she went round to her uncle's house.

Before leaving for the Orinoco, Uncle Hamish helped his niece settle the alligator comfortably in the wheelchair, packing it in with lots of wet cushions. The big sun bonnet nearly hid its snout, but Marilyn made it wear sunglasses to help the disguise.

'I shan't forget this,' Sir Hamish said in a deeply grateful voice.

'Neither shall I,' murmured Marilyn, wheeling the alligator out into the street.

As Marilyn pushed the disguised alligator through her front gate she noticed Archie Lightfoot pushing a large motorized wheelchair through his front gate, too. Sitting in it was someone muffled in a scarf, a floppy hat and sunglasses.

'My old grandfather is coming to live with me for a while,' Archie said with a nervous laugh.

'How funny!' said Marilyn. 'My old granny is coming to stay with *me*.'

The two old grandparents looked at each other through their sunglasses and grinned toothily.

'Unfortunately,' Archie added quickly, 'my old grandfather can sometimes be very crabby. He has a big heart, but occasionally he works himself up into a bad temper. Do warn your grandmother not to talk to him.'

'I have the same problem with Granny,' Marilyn replied. 'She is basically big-hearted, but at times she can be bad-tempered. If you try to talk to her when she's hungry, she just snaps your head off!'

At first, things went smoothly. Every day Marilyn gave the alligator a large breakfast of fish and tomato sauce. Then she tucked the huge reptile into the wheelchair with blankets soaked in home-made mud. Next, she wheeled it into the garden and settled it down with a bottle of cordial, an open tin of sardines and the newspaper. The alligator always looked eagerly over the fence to see what was going on next door.

In his garden, Archie Lightfoot was settling his old grandfather down with tuna-fish sandwiches and a motoring magazine. His

grandfather blew a daring kiss to Marilyn
Hawthorn's grandmother. Marilyn
saw her alligator blow one back.

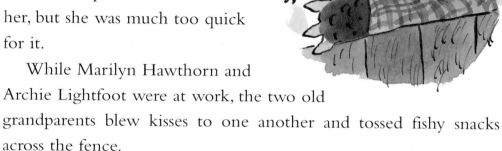

'You are not to blow kisses to
a respectable old gentleman,' she
said sternly. The grandfather
blew another kiss and the
alligator did the same. Marilyn
smacked its paw. It tried to bite
her, but she was much too quick
for it.

While Marilyn Hawthorn and
Archie Lightfoot were at work, the two old
grandparents blew kisses to one another and tossed fishy snacks
across the fence.

That evening, when Marilyn Hawthorn got home, she noticed
that her alligator seemed rather ill. It sighed a great deal, and
merely toyed with its sardines at supper. Marilyn felt its forehead. It
was warm and feverish, a bad thing in alligators, which are, of
course, cold-blooded. She took it to the vet at once.

'What on earth is this?' cried the vet, listening to the alligator's
heart. 'This alligator is in love!'

The alligator sighed so deeply it accidentally swallowed the vet's
thermometer.

'It must be homesick for the Orinoco,' Marilyn thought to
herself. So she took a day off work, wrapped cool mud-packs
around the alligator, and put it in the marigold garden – with a large
photograph of the Orinoco river to look at.

As she was doing this, Archie Lightfoot's face appeared over the garden fence.

'Oh, I'm so worried about my grandfather,' he cried. 'I have had to take him to the vet – I mean, the doctor – and he sighed so deeply that he swallowed a stethoscope.'

'And I've had to take the day off work to look after my old granny,' said Marilyn. 'She has swallowed a thermometer.'

'Ahem!' coughed Archie Lightfoot, clearing his throat nervously. 'Perhaps, since you are taking the day off work, you might like to slip over and see my stamp collection.'

'I'd love to,' replied Marilyn.

Marilyn Hawthorn and Archie Lightfoot spent rather a long time looking at the stamp collection. They forgot their responsibilities. But when they switched on the radio, they were alarmed to hear the following announcement:

'We interrupt this programme to bring you horrifying news. Two twenty-foot saurians – crocodiles, or perhaps they are alligators – both wearing sunglasses, are driving down the main road in motorized wheelchairs.'

'Oh, no!' cried Archie Lightfoot.

'Oh, no!' cried Marilyn Hawthorn.

Together, they ran outside. Their two lawns were quite empty.

'This is serious,' gasped Marilyn. 'Oh, Mr Lightfoot, I must confess that my grandmother is really an alligator!'

'And my old grandfather's a crocodile,' cried Archie. 'I didn't dream that a lovely woman like you could be fond of reptiles.'

'We can discuss that later,' said Marilyn briskly. 'First, we must get our dear pets back.'

Quickly, they climbed into Marilyn's sports car and took off after the runaway reptiles. They soon saw them whizzing along in their wheelchairs. Overhead, a police helicopter hovered, with several policemen and the vet inside it.

'It's very strange,' said Marilyn, 'but they seem to be heading for my uncle's house. I do wish Uncle Hamish were at home. He would know what to do in a case like this.'

The runaways turned into the street where Marilyn's uncle lived, but they did not turn in at his gate. Instead, they went through the next-door gateway, straight to the home of the Reverend Crabtree.

Imagine Marilyn's surprise when she saw her Uncle Hamish sitting on the veranda, showing the Reverend Crabtree his souvenirs of the Orinoco.

'Uncle, I didn't know you were back!' she exclaimed.

'Well, I have only just returned,' he said, looking in amazement at the two reptiles. 'The Orinoco wasn't as good as I remembered it, so I came home early. But Marilyn, why has my alligator split itself in two?'

'Oh, Uncle, this is not another alligator — it's a crocodile. And it belongs to Archie Lightfoot,' Marilyn explained. 'These two bad reptiles ran away together in their wheelchairs and came here.'

By now the police helicopter had landed on the lawn, and the policemen, followed by the vet, came running over.

'Don't hurt those saurians,' the vet was shouting. 'They are not very well. They are in love!'

'Ah,' said the Reverend Crabtree. 'I understand! They have

eloped and wish to get married.'

The crocodile and the alligator swished their tails and snapped their jaws as one reptile, to show he was right.

'I'm not sure if I, a minister of the church, should marry an alligator and a crocodile,' said the Reverend Crabtree doubtfully. 'It doesn't seem very respectable.'

'But it seems a pity to miss out on the chance of marrying two creatures so clearly in love,' said Archie. Then, turning to Marilyn, he added, 'Suppose we get married, too. Will that make it more respectable? After all, we did bring these two reptiles together. It's only fair that they should do the same for us!'

So Marilyn Hawthorn married Archie Lightfoot, and the crocodile and alligator were married too. Sir Hamish gave both brides away. Then he swapped over and became best man to the two bridegrooms.

Marilyn and Archie turned their two little houses into one large house, and their lawns into a swimming-pool for the two saurians. And they lived happily ever after, even though they had to begin every morning of their lives together feeding sardines to a handsome Nile crocodile and an Orinoco alligator – both with big hearts and even bigger appetites.

Rudyard Kipling

JUST SO STORIES

ILLUSTRATED BY MIKE TERRY

HOW THE CAMEL GOT HIS HUMP

NOW this is the next tale, and it tells how the Camel got his big hump.

In the beginning of years, when the world was so new-and-all, and the Animals were just beginning to work for Man, there was a Camel, and he lived in the middle of a Howling Desert because he did not want to work; and besides, he was a Howler himself. So he ate sticks and thorns and tamarisks and milkweed and prickles, most 'scruciating idle; and when anybody spoke to him he said, 'Humph!' Just 'Humph!' and no more.

Presently the Horse came to him on Monday morning, with a saddle on his back and a bit in his mouth, and said, 'Camel, O Camel, come out and trot like the rest of us.'

'Humph!' said the Camel; and the Horse went away and told the Man.

Presently the Dog came to him, with a stick in his mouth, and said, 'Camel, O Camel, come and fetch and carry like the rest of us.'

'Humph!' said the Camel; and the Dog went away and told the Man.

Presently the Ox came to him, with the yoke on his neck, and said, 'Camel, O Camel, come and plough like the rest of us.'

'Humph!' said the Camel; and the Ox went away and told the Man.

At the end of the day the Man called the Horse and the Dog and the Ox together, and said, 'Three, O Three, I'm very sorry for you (with the world so new-and-all); but that Humph-thing in the Desert can't work, or he would

have been here by now, so I am going to leave him alone, and you must work double-time to make up for it.'

That made the Three very angry (with the world so new-and-all), and they held a palaver, and an *indaba*, and a *punchayet*, and a pow-wow on the edge of the Desert; and the Camel came chewing milkweed *most* 'scruciating idle, and laughed at them. Then he said 'Humph!' and went away again.

Presently there came along the Djinn in charge of All Deserts, rolling in a cloud of dust (Djinns always travel that way because it is Magic), and he stopped to palaver and pow-wow with the Three.

'Djinn of All Deserts,' said the Horse, 'is it right for any one to be idle, with the world so new-and-all?'

'Certainly not,' said the Djinn.

'Well,' said the Horse, 'there's a thing in the middle of your Howling Desert (and he's a Howler himself) with a long neck and long legs, and he hasn't done a stroke of work since Monday morning. He won't trot.'

'Whew!' said the Djinn, whistling, 'that's my Camel, for all the gold in Arabia! What does he say about it?'

'He says "Humph!"' said the Dog; 'and he won't fetch and carry.'

'Does he say anything else?'

'Only "Humph!"; and he won't plough,' said the Ox.

'Very good,' said the Djinn. 'I'll humph him if you will kindly wait a minute.'

The Djinn rolled himself up in his dustcloak, and took a bearing across the desert, and found the Camel most 'scruciatingly idle, looking at his own reflection in a pool of water.

'My long and bubbling friend,' said the Djinn, 'what's this I hear of your doing no work, with the world so new-and-all?'

'Humph!' said the Camel.

The Djinn sat down, with his chin in his hand, and began to think a Great Magic, while the Camel looked at his own reflection in the pool of water.

'You've given the Three extra work ever since Monday morning, all on account of your 'scruciating idleness,' said the Djinn; and he went on thinking Magics, with his chin in his hand.

'Humph!' said the Camel.

'I shouldn't say that again if I were you,' said the Djinn; 'you might say it once too often. Bubbles, I want you to work.'

And the Camel said 'Humph!' again; but no sooner had he said it than he saw his back, that he was so proud of, puffing up and

puffing up into a great big lolloping humph.

'Do you see that?' said the Djinn. 'That's your very own humph that you've brought upon your very own self by not working. Today is Thursday, and you've done no work since Monday, when the work began. Now you are going to work.'

'How can I,' said the Camel, 'with this humph on my back?'

'That's made a-purpose,' said the Djinn, 'all because you missed those three days. You will be able to work now for three days without eating, because you can live on your humph; and don't you ever say I never did anything for you. Come out of the Desert and go to the Three, and behave. Humph yourself!'

And the Camel humphed himself, humph and all, and went away to join the Three. And from that day to this the Camel always wears a humph (we call it 'hump' now, not to hurt his feelings); but he has never yet caught up with the three days that he missed at the beginning of the world, and he has never yet learned how to behave.

Louisa May Alcott

LITTLE WOMEN

ILLUSTRATED BY EMMA CHICHESTER CLARK

JO MEETS APOLLYON

The four March girls, Meg, Jo, Beth and Amy, are growing up at the time
of the American Civil War. Although their father is away with the army
and they are quite poor, they are a happy family. But in this extract Jo
and Amy have a really dreadful quarrel.

'GIRLS, where are you going?' asked Amy, coming into their room one Saturday afternoon, and finding them getting ready to go out, with an air of secrecy, which excited her curiosity.

'Never mind; little girls shouldn't ask questions,' returned Jo, sharply.

Now if there *is* anything mortifying to our feelings, when we are young, it is to be told that; and to be bidden to 'run away, dear', is still more trying to us. Amy bridled up at this insult, and determined to find out the secret, if she teased for an hour. Turning to Meg, who never refused her anything very long, she said coaxingly, 'Do tell me!

I should think you might let me go too; for Beth is fussing over her piano, and I haven't got anything to do, and am *so* lonely.'

'I can't, dear, because you aren't invited,' began Meg; but Jo broke in impatiently, 'Now, Meg, be quiet, or you will spoil it all. You can't go, Amy; so don't be a baby and whine about it.'

'You are going somewhere with Laurie, I know you are; you were whispering and laughing together, on the sofa, last night, and you stopped when I came in. Aren't you going with him?'

'Yes, we are; now do be still and stop bothering.'

Amy held her tongue, but used her eyes, and saw Meg slip a fan into her pocket.

'I know! I know! You're going to the hall to see "The Seven Castles"!' she cried, adding resolutely, 'and I *shall* go, for Mother said I might see it; and I've got my rag-money, and it was mean not to tell me in time.'

'Just listen to me a minute, and be a good child,' said Meg, soothingly. 'Mother doesn't wish you to go this week, because your eyes are not well enough yet to bear the light of this fairy piece. Next week you can go with Beth and Hannah, and have a nice time.'

'I don't like that half as well as going with you and Laurie. Please let me; I've been sick with this cold for so long, and shut up, I'm dying for some fun. Do, Meg! I'll be ever so good,' pleaded Amy, looking as pathetic as she could.

'Suppose we take her. I don't believe Mother would mind, if we bundle her up well,' began Meg.

'If *she* goes *I* shan't; and if I don't, Laurie won't like it; and it will be very rude, after he invited only us, to go and drag in Amy. I

should think she'd hate to poke herself where she isn't wanted,' said Jo, crossly, for she disliked the trouble of overseeing a fidgety child, when she wanted to enjoy herself.

Her tone and manner angered Amy, who began to put her boots on, saying, in her most aggravating way, 'I *shall* go; Meg says I may; and if I pay for myself, Laurie hasn't anything to do with it.'

'You can't sit with us, for our seats are reserved, and you mustn't sit alone; so Laurie will give you his place, and that will spoil our pleasure; or he'll get another seat for you, and that isn't proper, when you weren't asked. You shan't stir a step; so you may just have to stay where you are,' scolded Jo, crosser than ever, having just pricked her finger in her hurry.

Sitting on the floor, with one boot on, Amy began to cry, and

Meg to reason with her, when Laurie called from below, and the two girls hurried down, leaving their sister wailing; for now and then she forgot her grown-up ways, and acted like a spoilt child. Just as the party were setting out, Amy called over the banisters, in a threatening voice, 'You'll be sorry for this, Jo March; see if you ain't.'

'Fiddlesticks!' returned Jo, slamming the door.

They had a charming time, for 'The Seven Castles of the Diamond Lake' was as brilliant and wonderful as heart could wish. But, in spite of the comical red imps, sparkling elves, and gorgeous princes and princesses, Jo's pleasure had a drop of bitterness in it; the fairy queen's yellow curls reminded her of Amy; and between the acts she amused herself with wondering what her sister would do to make her 'sorry for it'. She and Amy had had many lively skirmishes in the course of their lives, for both had quick tempers, and were apt to be violent when fairly roused. Amy teased Jo, Jo irritated Amy, and semi-occasional explosions occurred, of which both were much ashamed afterwards. Although the oldest, Jo had the least self-control, and had hard times trying to curb the fiery spirit which was continually getting her into trouble; her anger never lasted long, and having humbly confessed her fault she sincerely repented and tried to do better. Her sisters used to say that they rather liked to get Jo into a fury because she was such an angel afterwards. Poor Jo tried desperately to be good, but her bosom enemy was always ready to flame up and defeat her; and it took years of patient effort to subdue it.

When they got home they found Amy reading in the parlour. She assumed an injured air as they came in; never lifted her eyes from her book, or asked a single question. Perhaps curiosity might have conquered resentment, if Beth had not been there to inquire, and receive a glowing description of the play. On going up to put away her best hat, Jo's first look was towards the bureau; for, in their last quarrel, Amy had soothed her feelings by turning Jo's top drawer upside down on the floor. Everything was in its place, however, and after a hasty glance into her various closets, bags, and boxes, Jo decided that Amy had forgiven and forgotten her wrongs.

There Jo was mistaken; for next day she made a discovery which produced a tempest. Meg, Beth, and Amy were sitting together, late in the afternoon, when Jo burst into the room, looking excited, and demanding breathlessly, 'Has anyone taken my book?'

Meg and Beth said 'No,' at once, and looked surprised; Amy poked the fire, and said nothing. Jo saw her colour rise, and was down upon her in a minute.

'Amy, you've got it.'

'No, I haven't.'

'You know where it is, then!'

'No, I don't.'

'That's a fib!' cried Jo, taking her by the shoulders and looking fierce enough to frighten a much braver child than Amy.

'It isn't. I haven't got it, don't know where it is now, and don't care.'

'You know something about it, and you'd better tell at once, or I'll make you,' and Jo gave her a slight shake.

'Scold as much as you like, you'll never see your silly old book again,' cried Amy, getting excited in her turn.

'Why not?'

'I burnt it up.'

'What! My little book I was so fond of, and worked over, and meant to finish before Father got home! Have you really burnt it?' said Jo, turning very pale, while her eyes kindled and her hands clutched Amy nervously.

'Yes, I did! I told you I'd make you pay for being so cross yesterday, and I have, so –'

Amy got no further, for Jo's hot temper mastered her, and she shook Amy till her teeth chattered in her head; crying in a passion of grief and anger:

'You wicked, wicked girl! I never can write it again and I'll never forgive you as long as I live.'

Meg flew to rescue Amy, and Beth to pacify Jo, but Jo was quite beside herself; and with a parting box on her sister's ear, she rushed out of the room up to the old sofa in the garret, and finished her fight alone.

The storm cleared up below, for Mrs March came home, and, having heard the story, soon brought Amy to a sense of the wrong she had done her sister. Jo's book was the pride of her heart, and was regarded by her family as a literary sprout of great promise. It was only half a dozen little fairy tales, but Jo had worked over them patiently, putting her whole heart into her work hoping to make something good enough to print. She had just copied them with great care, and had destroyed the old manuscript, so that Amy's bonfire had consumed the loving work of several years. It seemed a small loss to others, but to Jo it was a dreadful calamity, and she felt that it never could be made up to her. Beth mourned as for a departed kitten, and Meg refused to defend her pet; Mrs March looked grave and grieved, and Amy felt that no one would love her till she had asked pardon for the act which she now regretted more than any of them.

When the tea-bell rang Jo appeared, looking so grim and unapproachable, that it took all Amy's courage to say meekly:

'Please forgive me, Jo; I'm very, very sorry.'

'I never shall forgive you,' was Jo's stern answer; and from that moment she ignored Amy entirely.

No one spoke of the great trouble – not even Mrs March – for all had learned by experience that when Jo was in that mood words were wasted; and the wisest course was to wait till some little accident, or her own generous nature, softened Jo's resentment, and healed the breach. It was not a happy evening; for though they sewed as usual, while their mother read aloud from Bremer, Scott, or Edgeworth, something was wanting and the sweet home peace was disturbed. They felt this most when singing time came; for Beth could only play, Jo stood dumb as stone, and Amy broke down, so Meg and Mother sang alone. But in spite of their efforts to be as cheery as larks, the flute-like voices did not seem to chord as well as usual, and all felt out of tune.

As Jo received her good-night kiss, Mrs March whispered gently: 'My dear, don't let the sun go down upon your anger; forgive each other, help each other, and begin again tomorrow.'

Jo wanted to lay her head down on that motherly bosom, and cry her grief and anger all away, but tears were an unmanly weakness, and she felt so deeply injured that she really *couldn't* quite forgive yet. So she winked hard, shook her head, and said gruffly, because Amy was listening: 'It was an abominable thing, and she don't deserve to be forgiven.'

With that she marched off to bed, and there was no merry or confidential gossip that night.

T. H. White

THE ONCE AND FUTURE KING

ILLUSTRATED BY PAULINE BAYNES

THE SWORD IN THE STONE

*Merlyn the magician has taught the young King Arthur many things by
turning him into different animals. Now Arthur, nicknamed the Wart,
faces his first great trial.*

LONDON was full to the brim. If Sir Ector had not been
lucky enough to own a little land in Pie Street, on which
there stood a respectable inn, they would have been hard put
to it to find a lodging. But he did own it, and as a matter of fact drew
most of his dividends from that source, so they were able to get three
beds between the five of them. They thought themselves fortunate.

On the first day of the tournament, Sir Kay managed to get them
on the way to the lists at least an hour before the jousts could
possibly begin. He had lain awake all night imagining how he was
going to beat the best barons in England, and he had not been able

to eat his breakfast. Now he rode at the front of the cavalcade, with pale cheeks, and the Wart wished there was something he could do to calm him down.

For country people, who only knew the dismantled tilting ground of Sir Ector's castle, the scene which met their eyes was ravishing. It was a huge green pit in the earth, about as big as the arena at a football match. It lay ten feet lower than the surrounding country, with sloping banks, and the snow had been swept off it. It had been kept warm with straw, which had been cleared off that morning, and now the close-worn grass sparkled green in the white landscape. Round the arena there was a world of colour so dazzling and moving and twinkling as to make one blink one's eyes. The wooden grandstands were painted in scarlet and white. The silk

pavilions of famous people, pitched on every side, were azure and green and saffron and chequered. The pennons and pennoncels which floated everywhere in the sharp wind were flapping with every colour of the rainbow, as they strained and slapped at their flag-poles, and the barrier down the middle of the arena itself was done in chessboard squares of black and white. Most of the combatants and their friends had not yet arrived, but one could see from those few who had come how the very people would turn the scene into a bank of flowers, and how the armour would flash, and the scalloped sleeves of the heralds jig in the wind, as they raised their brazen trumpets to their lips to shake the fleecy clouds of winter with joyances and fanfares.

'Good heavens!' cried Sir Kay. 'I have left my sword at home.'

'Can't joust without a sword,' said Sir Grummore. 'Quite irregular.'

'Better go and fetch it,' said Sir Ector. 'You have time.'

'My squire will do it,' said Sir Kay. 'What a damned mistake to make! Here, squire, ride hard back to the inn and fetch my sword. You shall have a shilling if you fetch it in time.'

The Wart went as pale as Sir Kay was, and looked as if he were going to strike him. Then he said, 'It shall be done, master,' and turned his ambling palfrey against the stream of newcomers. He began to push his way towards their hostelry as best he might.

'To offer me money!' cried the Wart to himself. 'To look down at this beastly little donkey-affair off his great charger and to call me Squire! Oh, Merlyn, give me patience with the brute, and stop me from throwing his filthy shilling in his face.'

When he got to the inn it was closed. Everybody had thronged to see the famous tournament, and the entire household had followed after the mob. Those were lawless days and it was not safe to leave your house – or even to go to sleep in it – unless you were certain that it was impregnable. The wooden shutters bolted over the downstairs windows were two inches thick, and the doors were double-barred.

'Now what do I do,' asked the Wart, 'to earn my shilling?'

He looked ruefully at the blind little inn, and began to laugh.

'Poor Kay,' he said. 'All that shilling stuff was only because he was scared and miserable, and now he has good cause to be. Well, he shall have a sword of some sort if I have to break into the Tower of London.

'How does one get hold of a sword?' he continued. 'Where can I steal one? Could I waylay some knight, even if I am mounted on an ambling pad, and take his weapon by force? There must be some swordsmith or armourer in a great town like this, whose shop would be still open.'

He turned his mount and cantered off down the street. There was a quiet churchyard at the end of it, with a kind of square in front of the church door. In the middle of the square there was a heavy stone with an anvil on it, and a fine new sword was stuck through the anvil.

'Well,' said the Wart, 'I suppose it is some sort of war memorial, but it will have to do. I am sure nobody would grudge Kay a war memorial, if they knew his desperate straits.'

He tied his reins round a post of the lych-gate, strode up the gravel path, and took hold of the sword.

'Come, sword,' he said. 'I must cry your mercy and take you for a better cause.

'This is extraordinary,' said the Wart. 'I feel strange when I have hold of this sword, and I notice everything much more clearly. Look at the beautiful gargoyles of the church, and of the monastery which it belongs to. See how splendidly all the famous banners in the aisle are waving. How nobly that yew holds up the red flakes of its timbers to worship God. How clean the snow is. I can smell something like feverfew and sweet briar – and is it music that I hear?'

It was music, whether of pan-pipes or of recorders, and the light in the churchyard was so clear, without being dazzling, that one could have picked a pin out twenty yards away.

'There is something in this place,' said the Wart. 'There are people. Oh, people, what do you want?'

Nobody answered him, but the music was loud and the light beautiful.

'People,' cried the Wart, 'I must take this sword. It is not for me, but for Kay. I will bring it back.'

There was still no answer, and the Wart turned back to the anvil. He saw the golden letters, which he did not read, and the jewels on the pommel, flashing in the lovely light.

'Come, sword,' said the Wart. He took hold of the handles with both hands, and strained against the stone. There was a melodious consort on the recorders, but nothing moved.

The Wart let go of the handles, when they were beginning to bite into the palms of his hands, and stepped back, seeing stars.

'It is well fixed,' he said.

He took hold of it again and pulled with all his might. The music played more strongly, and the light all about the churchyard glowed like amethysts; but the sword still stuck.

'Oh, Merlyn,' cried the Wart, 'help me to get this weapon.'

There was a kind of rushing noise, and a long chord played along with it. All round the churchyard there were hundreds of old friends. They rose over the church wall all together, like the Punch and Judy ghosts of remembered days, and there were badgers and nightingales and vulgar crows and hares and wild geese and falcons and fishes and

dogs and dainty unicorns and solitary wasps and corkindrills and hedgehogs and griffins and the thousand other animals he had met. They loomed round the church wall, the lovers and helpers of the Wart, and they all spoke solemnly in turn. Some of them had come from the banners in the church, where they were painted in heraldry, some from the waters and the sky and the fields about – but all, down to the smallest shrew mouse, had come to help on account of love. The Wart felt his power grow.

'Put your back into it,' said a Luce (or pike) off one of the heraldic banners, 'as you once did when I was going to snap you up. Remember that power springs from the nape of the neck.'

'What about those forearms,' asked a badger gravely, 'that are held together by a chest? Come along, my dear embryo, and find your tool.'

A Merlin sitting at the top of the yew tree cried out, 'Now then, Captain Wart, what is the first law of the foot? I thought I once heard something about never letting go?'

'Don't work like a stalling woodpecker,' urged a Tawny Owl affectionately. 'Keep up a steady effort, my duck, and you will have it yet.'

A white-front said, 'Now, Wart, if you were once able to fly the great North Sea, surely you can co-ordinate a few little wing-muscles here and there? Fold your powers together, with the spirit of your mind, and it will come out like butter. Come along, Homo sapiens, for all we humble friends of yours are waiting here to cheer.'

The Wart walked up to the great sword for the third time. He put out his right hand softly and drew it out as gently as from a scabbard.

∾

Joan Aiken

HUMBLEPUPPY

ILLUSTRATED BY TONY ROSS

OUR house was furnished mainly from auction sales. When you buy furniture that way you get a lot of extra things besides the particular piece that you were after, because the stuff is sold in lots: *Lot 13, two Persian rugs, a set of golf-clubs, a sewing-machine, a walnut radio-cabinet, and a plinth.*

It was in this way that I acquired a tin deedbox, which came with two coal-scuttles and a broom cupboard. The deedbox is solid metal, painted black, big as a medium-sized suitcase. When I first brought it home I put it in my study, planning to use it as a kind of filing-cabinet for old typescripts. I had gone into the kitchen, and was

arranging the brooms in their new home, when I heard a muffled thumping coming from the study. I went back, thinking that a bird must have flown in through the window; no bird, but the thumping seemed to be inside

the deedbox. I had already opened it to see if there were any diamonds or bearer bonds worth thousands of pounds inside (there weren't), but now I opened it again. The key was attached to the handle by a thin chain. There was nothing inside. I shut it. The noise started again. I opened it. Still nothing inside.

Well, this was broad daylight, two o'clock on Thursday afternoon, people going past in the road outside and a radio schools programme chatting away to itself in the next room. It was not a ghostly kind of time, so I put my hand into the empty box and moved it about.

Something shrank away from my hand. I heard a faint, scared whimper. It could almost have been my own, but wasn't. Knowing that someone – something? – else was afraid too put heart into me. Exploring carefully and gently around the interior of the box, I felt the contour of a small, bony, warm, trembling body with big awkward feet, silky dangling ears, and a cold nose that, when I found it, nudged for a moment anxiously but trustingly into the palm of my hand.

So I knelt down, put the other hand into the box as well, cupped them under a thin little ribby chest, and lifted out – Humblepuppy. He was quite light.

I couldn't see him, but I could hear his faint inquiring whimper, and I could hear his toenails scratching on the floorboards.

Just at that moment the cat, Taffy, came in.

Taffy has a lot of character. Every cat has a lot of character, but Taffy has more than most, all of it inconvenient. For instance, although he is very sociable, and longs for company, he just despises company in the form of dogs. The mere sound of a dog

barking two streets away is enough to make his fur stand up like a porcupine's quills and his tail swell like a mushroom cloud.

Which it did the instant he saw Humblepuppy.

Now here is the interesting thing. *I* could feel and hear Humblepuppy, but couldn't see him; *Taffy*, apparently, could see and smell him, but couldn't feel him. We soon discovered this. For Taffy, sinking into a low, gladiatorial crouch, letting out all the time a fearsome throaty wailing, like a bagpipe revving up its drone, inched his way along to where Humblepuppy huddled trembling by my left foot, and then dealt him what ought to have been a swinging right-handed clip on the ear. 'Get out of my house, you filthy little canine scum!' was what he was plainly intending to convey.

But the swipe failed to connect; instead it landed on my shin.

I've never seen a cat so astonished. It was like watching a kitten meet itself for the first time in a looking-glass. Taffy ran round to the back of where Humblepuppy was sitting; felt; smelt; poked gingerly

48

with a paw; leapt back nervously; crept forward again. All the time Humblepuppy just sat, trembling a little, giving out this faint beseeching sound that meant: 'I'm only a poor little mongrel without a smidgeon of harm in me. *Please* don't do anything nasty! I don't even know how I came here.'

It certainly was a puzzle how he had come. I rang the auctioneers (after shutting Taffy *out* and Humblepuppy *into* the study with a bowl of water and a handful of Boniebisk, Taffy's favourite breakfast food).

The auctioneers told me that *Lot 12, Deedbox, coal-scuttles and broom cupboard*, had come from Riverland Rectory, where Mr Smythe, the old rector, had lately died aged ninety. Had he ever possessed a dog, or a puppy? They couldn't say; they had merely received instructions from a firm of lawyers to sell the furniture.

I never did discover how poor little Humblepuppy's ghost got into that deedbox. Maybe he was shut in by mistake, long ago;

maybe some callous Victorian gardener dropped him, box and all, into a river, and the box was later found.

Anyway, and whatever had happened in the past, now that Humblepuppy had come out of his box he was very ready to be grateful and affectionate. As I sat typing I'd often hear a patter-patter, and feel his small chin fit itself comfortably over my foot, ears dangling. Goodness knows what kind of a mixture he was; something between a spaniel and a terrier, I'd guess. In the evening, watching television or sitting by the fire, one would suddenly find his warm weight leaning against one's leg. (He didn't put on a lot of weight, but his bony little ribs filled out a bit.)

For the first few weeks we had a lot of trouble with Taffy, who was very surly over the whole business and blamed me bitterly for not getting rid of this low-class intruder. But Humblepuppy was extremely placating, got back into his deedbox whenever the atmosphere became too volcanic, and did his very best not to be a nuisance.

By and by Taffy thawed. As I've said, he is really a very sociable cat. Although quite old, seventy cat years, he dearly likes cheerful company, and generally has some young cat friend who comes to play with him. In the last few years we've had Whisky, the black-and-white pub cat, who used to sit washing the smell of fish-and-chips off his fur under the dripping tap in our kitchen sink; Tetanus, the hairdresser's thick-set black, who took a fancy to sleeping on top of our china cupboard every night, and used to startle me very much by jumping down heavily on to my shoulder as I made the breakfast coffee; Sweet Charity, a little grey Persian who came to a sad end under the wheels of a police car, and Charity's

grey-and-white stripy cousin Fred, whose owners presently moved from next door to another part of the town.

It was soon after Fred's departure that Humblepuppy arrived, and from my point of view he couldn't have been more welcome. Taffy missed Fred badly, and expected *me* to play with him instead; it was sad to see this large elderly tabby rushing hopefully up and down the stairs after breakfast, or hiding behind the armchair and jumping out on to nobody; or howling, howling, howling at me till I escorted him out into the garden where he'd rush to the lavender bush which had been the traditional hiding-place of Whisky, Tetanus, Charity, and Fred in succession.

So sometimes, on a working morning, I'd be at my wits' end, almost on the point of going across the town to our ex-neighbours, ringing the bell, and saying, 'Please can Fred come and play?'

Specially on a rainy, uninviting day, when Taffy was pacing gloomily about the house with drooping head and switching tail, grumbling about the weather and the lack of company, and blaming me for both. Humblepuppy's arrival changed all that.

At first Taffy considered it necessary to police him, and that kept him fully occupied for hours. He'd sit on guard by the deedbox till Humblepuppy woke up in the morning, and then he'd follow officiously all over the house. Humblepuppy was slow and cautious in his explorations, but by degrees he picked up courage and found his way into every corner. He never once made a puddle; he learned to use Taffy's cat-flap and go out into the garden, though he was always more timid outside and would scamper for home at any loud noise. Planes and cars terrified him, which made me still more certain that he had been in that deedbox for a long, long time, since before such things were invented.

Presently he learned, or Taffy taught him, to hide in the lavender bush like Whisky, Charity, Tetanus, and Fred; and the two of them used to play their own ghostly version of touch-last for hours on end.

When visitors came, Humblepuppy always retired to his deedbox; he was decidedly scared of strangers; which made his behaviour with Mr Manningham, the new rector of Riverland, all the more surprising.

As I was dying to learn anything I could of the old rectory's history, I'd invited Mr Manningham to tea. He was a thin, gentle, quiet man, who had done missionary work in the Far East and had fallen ill and had had to come back to England. He seemed a little sad and lonely. I liked him. He told me that for a large part of the

53

nineteenth century the Riverland living had belonged to a parson called the Reverend Timothy Swannett, who had lived to a great age and had had ten children.

'He was a great-uncle of mine as a matter of fact. But why do you want to know all this?' Mr Manningham asked. His long thin arm hung over the side of his chair; absently he moved his hand sideways and remarked, 'I didn't know you had a puppy.' Then he looked down and said, 'Oh!'

'He's never come out for a stranger before,' I said.

Humblepuppy climbed invisibly on to Mr Manningham's lap.

We agreed that the new rector probably carried a familiar smell of his rectory with him, or possibly he reminded Humblepuppy of his great-uncle the Rev. Swannett. Anyway, after that, Humblepuppy always came scampering joyfully out if Mr Manningham dropped in to tea, so of course I thought of the rector when summer holiday time came round.

During the summer holiday we lend our house and cat to a lady publisher and her mother who are devoted to cats and think it a privilege to look after Taffy and spoil him. He is always amazingly overweight when we get back. But the old lady has an allergy to dogs, and is frightened of them too, so it was plainly out of the question that she should be expected to share her summer holiday with the ghost of a puppy.

So I asked Mr Manningham if he'd be prepared to take Humblepuppy as a boarder, since it didn't seem a case for the usual kind of boarding-kennels; he said he'd be delighted.

I drove Humblepuppy out to Riverland in his deedbox; he was rather miserable on the drive but luckily it is not far. Mr

Manningham came out into the garden to meet me. We put the box down on the lawn and opened it.

I've never heard a puppy so wildly excited. Often I'd been sorry that I couldn't see Humblepuppy, but I was never sorrier than on that afternoon, as we heard him rushing from tree to familiar tree, barking joyously, dashing through the orchard grass – you could see it divide as he whizzed along – coming back to bounce up against us, all damp and earthy and smelling of leaves.

'He's going to be happy with you all right,' I said, and Mr Manningham's grey, lined face crinkled into its thoughtful smile as he said, 'It's the place more than me, I think.' Well, it was both of them really.

When the holiday was over I went round to collect Humblepuppy, leaving Taffy haughty and standoffish, sniffing our cases. It always takes him a long time to forgive us for going away.

Mr Manningham had a bit of a cold and was sitting by the fire in his study, wrapped in a Shetland rug. Humblepuppy was on his knee. I could hear the little dog's tail thump against the arm of the chair when I walked in, but he didn't get down to greet me. He stayed in Mr Manningham's lap.

'So you've come to take back my boarder,' Mr Manningham said.

There was nothing in the least strained about his voice or smile but – I just hadn't the heart to take back Humblepuppy. I put my hand down, found his soft wrinkly forehead, rumpled it a bit, and said, 'Well – I was sort of wondering; our spoilt old cat seems to have got used to being on his own again and I was wondering whether – by any chance – you'd feel like keeping him?'

Mr Manningham's face lit up. He didn't speak for a minute, then he put a gentle hand down and rubbed a finger along Humble-puppy's chin.

'Well,' he said. He cleared his throat. 'Of course, if you're *quite* sure . . .'

'Quite sure.' My throat needed clearing too.

'I hope you won't catch my cold,' said Mr Manningham.

I shook my head and said, 'I'll drop in to see if you're better in a day or two,' and went off and left them together.

Poor Taffy was pretty glum over the loss of his playmate for several weeks; we had two hours' purgatory every morning after breakfast while he hunted for Humblepuppy high and low. But gradually the memory faded and, thank goodness, now he has found a new friend, Little Grey Furry, a nephew, cousin, or other relative of Charity and Fred. Little Grey Furry has learned to play hide-and-seek in the lavender bush, and to use our cat-flap, and clean up whatever's in Taffy's food bowl, so all is well in that department.

But I still miss Humblepuppy. I miss his cold nose exploring the palm of my hand as I sit thinking, in the middle of a page, and his warm weight leaning against my ankle as he watches the TV commercials. And the scritch-scratch of his toenails on the dining-room floor and the flump, flump as he comes downstairs, and the small hollow on a cushion as he settles down with a sigh.

Oh well. I'll get over it, just as Taffy has. But I was wondering about putting an ad into 'Our Dogs', or 'Pets' Monthly':

Wanted, ghost of mongrel puppy. Warm welcome, loving home.
Any reasonable price paid.

It might be worth a try.

L. Frank Baum

THE WIZARD OF OZ

ILLUSTRATED BY CHRIS RIDDELL

THE RESCUE OF THE TIN WOODMAN

Dorothy has been transported by a tornado from her farm in Kansas to Munchkinland. The only person who can tell her how to get home is the Wizard of Oz, who lives in the Emerald City. On her way to see him, Dorothy is joined by some strange companions.

WHEN Dorothy awoke the sun was shining through the trees and Toto had long been out chasing birds around her. There was the Scarecrow, still standing patiently in his corner, waiting for her.

'We must go and search for water,' she said to him.

'Why do you need water?' he asked.

'To wash my face clean after the dust of the road, and to drink, so the dry bread will not stick in my throat.'

'It must be inconvenient to be made of

flesh,' said the Scarecrow, thoughtfully, 'for you must sleep, and eat and drink. However, you have brains, and it is worth a lot of bother to be able to think properly.'

They left the cottage and walked through the trees until they found a little spring of clear water, where Dorothy drank and bathed and ate her breakfast. She saw there was not much bread left in the basket, and the girl was thankful the Scarecrow did not have to eat anything, for there was scarcely enough for herself and Toto for the day.

When she had finished her meal, and was about to go back to the road of yellow brick, she was startled to hear a deep groan near by.

'What was that?' she asked, timidly.

'I cannot imagine,' replied the Scarecrow; 'but we can go and see.'

Just then another groan reached their ears, and the sound seemed to come from behind them. They turned and walked through the forest a few steps, when Dorothy discovered something shining in a ray of sunshine that fell between the trees. She ran to the place and then stopped short, with a cry of surprise.

One of the big trees had been partly chopped through, and standing beside it, with an uplifted axe in his hands, was a man made entirely of tin. His head and arms and legs were jointed upon his body, but he stood perfectly motionless, as if he could not stir at all.

Dorothy looked at him in amazement, and so did the Scarecrow, while Toto barked sharply and made a snap at the tin legs, which hurt his teeth.

'Did you groan?' asked Dorothy.

'Yes,' answered the tin man, 'I did. I've been groaning for more than a year, and no one has ever heard me before or come to help me.'

'What can I do for you?' she inquired softly, for she was moved by the sad voice in which the man spoke.

'Get an oil-can and oil my joints,' he answered. 'They are rusted so badly that I cannot move them at all; if I am well oiled I shall soon be all right again. You will find an oil-can on a shelf in my cottage.'

Dorothy at once ran back to the cottage and found the oil-can, and then she returned and asked, anxiously, 'Where are your joints?'

'Oil my neck, first,' replied the Tin Woodman. So she oiled it, and as it was quite badly rusted the Scarecrow took hold of the tin head and moved it gently from side to side until it worked freely, and then the man could turn it himself.

'Now oil the joints in my arms,' he said. And Dorothy oiled them

61

and the Scarecrow bent them carefully until they were quite free from rust and as good as new.

The Tin Woodman gave a sigh of satisfaction and lowered his axe, which he leaned against the tree.

'This is a great comfort,' he said. 'I have been holding that axe in the air ever since I rusted, and I'm glad to be able to put it down at last. Now, if you will oil the joints of my legs, I shall be all right once more.'

So they oiled his legs until he could move them freely; and he thanked them again and again for his release, for he seemed a very polite creature, and very grateful.

'I might have stood there always if you had not come along,' he

said; 'so you have certainly saved my life. How did you happen to be here?'

'We are on our way to the Emerald City, to see the great Oz,' she answered, 'and we stopped at your cottage to pass the night.'

'Why do you wish to see Oz?' he asked.

'I want him to send me back to Kansas; and the Scarecrow wants him to put a few brains into his head,' she replied.

The Tin Woodman appeared to think deeply for a moment. Then he said: 'Do you suppose Oz could give me a heart?'

'Why, I guess so,' Dorothy answered. 'It would be as easy as to give the Scarecrow brains.'

'True,' the Tin Woodman returned. 'So, if you will allow me to join your party, I will also go to the Emerald City and ask Oz to help me.'

'Come along,' said the Scarecrow heartily; and Dorothy added that she would be pleased to have his company. So the Tin Woodman shouldered his axe and they all passed through the forest until they came to the road that was paved with yellow brick.

The Tin Woodman had asked Dorothy to put the oil-can in her basket. 'For,' he said, 'if I should get caught in the rain, and rust again, I would need the oil-can badly.'

It was a bit of good luck to have their new comrade join the party, for soon after they had begun their journey again they came to a place where the trees and branches grew so thick over the road that the travellers could not pass. But the Tin Woodman set to work with his axe and chopped so well that soon he cleared a passage for the entire party.

Dorothy was thinking so earnestly as they walked along that she did not notice when the Scarecrow stumbled into a hole and rolled over to the side of the road. Indeed he was obliged to call to her to help him up again.

'Why didn't you walk around the hole?' asked the Tin Woodman.

'I don't know enough,' replied the Scarecrow cheerfully. 'My head is stuffed with straw, you know, and that is why I am going to Oz to ask him for some brains.'

'Oh, I see,' said the Tin Woodman. 'But, after all, brains are not the best things in the world.'

'Have you any?' inquired the Scarecrow.

'No, my head is quite empty,' answered the Woodman; 'but once I had brains, and a heart also; so, having tried them both, I should much rather have a heart.'

'And why is that?' asked the Scarecrow.

'I will tell you my story, and then you will know.'

So, while they were walking through the forest, the Tin Woodman told the following story:

'I was born the son of a woodman who chopped down trees in the forest and sold the wood for a living. When I grew up I too became a woodchopper, and after my father died I took care of my old mother as long as she lived. Then I made up my mind that instead of living alone I would marry, so that I might not become lonely.

'There was one of the Munchkin girls who was so beautiful that I soon grew to love her with all my heart. She, on her part, promised to marry me as soon as I could earn enough money to build a better house for her; so I set to work harder than ever. But the girl lived with an old woman who did not want her to marry anyone, for she was so lazy she wished the girl to remain with her and do

65

the cooking and the housework. So the old woman went to the Wicked Witch of the East, and promised her two sheep and a cow if she would prevent the marriage. Thereupon the Wicked Witch enchanted my axe, and when I was chopping away at my best one day, for I was anxious to get the new house and my wife as soon as possible, the axe slipped all at once and cut off my left leg.

'This at first seemed a great misfortune, for I knew a one-legged man could not do very well as a woodchopper. So I went to a tinsmith and had him make me a new leg out of tin. The leg worked very well, once I was used to it; but my action angered the Wicked Witch of the East, for she had promised the old woman I should not marry the pretty Munchkin girl. When I began chopping again my axe slipped and cut off my right leg. Again I went to the tinner, and again he made me a leg out of tin. After this the enchanted axe cut off my arms, one after the other; but, nothing daunted, I had them replaced with tin ones. The Wicked Witch then made the axe slip and cut off my head, and at first I thought that was the end of me. But the tinsmith happened to come along, and he made me a new head out of tin.

'I thought I had beaten the Wicked Witch then, and I worked harder than ever; but I little knew how cruel my enemy could be. She thought of a new way to kill my love for the beautiful Munchkin maiden, and made my axe slip again, so that it cut right through my body, splitting me into two halves. Once more the tinsmith came to my help and made me a body of tin, fastening my tin arms and legs and head to it, by means of joints, so that I could move around as well as ever. But, alas! I had now no heart, so that I lost all my love for the Munchkin girl, and did not care whether I married her or not. I suppose she is still living with the old woman, waiting for me to come after her.

'My body shone so brightly in the sun that I felt very proud of it and it did not matter now if my axe slipped, for it could not cut me. There was only one danger – that my joints would rust; but I kept an oil-can in my cottage and took care to oil myself whenever I needed it. However, there came a day when I forgot to do this, and, being caught in a rainstorm, before I thought of the danger my joints had rusted, and I was left to stand in the woods until you came to help me. It was a terrible thing to undergo, but during the year I stood there I had time to think that the greatest loss I had known was the loss of my heart. While I was in love I was the happiest man on earth; but no one can love who has not a heart, and so I am resolved to ask Oz to give me one. If he does, I will go back to the Munchkin maiden and marry her.'

Both Dorothy and the Scarecrow had been greatly interested in the story of the Tin Woodman, and now they knew why he was so anxious to get a new heart.

'All the same,' said the Scarecrow, 'I shall ask for brains instead of a heart; for a fool would not know what to do with a heart if he had one.'

'I shall take the heart,' returned the Tin Woodman, 'for brains do not make one happy, and happiness is the best thing in the world.'

∾

C. S. Lewis

THE LION, THE WITCH AND THE WARDROBE

ILLUSTRATED BY PAULINE BAYNES

EDMUND AND THE WARDROBE

Peter, Susan, Edmund and Lucy are evacuated to an old country house during the Second World War. Lucy is the first to discover that an old wardrobe in a spare room is the gateway to Narnia, a country in the power of the White Witch. At first no one believes Lucy, but then Edmund follows her and meets the wicked Queen.

'BUT what *are* you?' said the Queen again. 'Are you a great overgrown dwarf that has cut off his beard?'

'No, Your Majesty,' said Edmund, 'I never had a beard, I'm a boy.'

'A boy!' said she. 'Do you mean you are a Son of Adam?'

Edmund stood still, saying nothing. He was too confused by this time to understand what the question meant.

'I see you are an idiot, whatever else you may be,' said the Queen.

'Answer me, once and for all, or I shall lose my patience. Are you human?'

'Yes, Your Majesty,' said Edmund.

'And how, pray, did you come to enter my dominions?'

'Please, Your Majesty, I came in through a wardrobe.'

'A wardrobe? What do you mean?'

'I – I opened a door and just found myself here, Your Majesty,' said Edmund.

'Ha!' said the Queen, speaking more to herself than to him. 'A door. A door from the world of men! I have heard of such things. This may wreck all. But he is only one, and he is easily dealt with.' As she spoke these words she rose from her seat and looked Edmund full in the face, her eyes flaming; at the same moment she raised her wand. Edmund felt sure that she was going to do something dreadful but he seemed unable to move. Then, just as he gave himself up for lost, she appeared to change her mind.

'My poor child,' she said in quite a different voice, 'how cold you look! Come and sit with me here on the sledge and I will put my mantle round you and we will talk.'

Edmund did not like this arrangement at all but he dared not disobey; he stepped on to the sledge and sat at her feet, and she put a fold of her fur mantle round him and tucked it well in.

'Perhaps something hot to drink?' said the Queen. 'Should you like that?'

'Yes please, Your Majesty,' said Edmund, whose teeth were chattering.

The Queen took from somewhere among her wrappings a very small bottle which looked as if it were made of copper. Then, holding out her arm, she let one drop fall from it on the snow beside the sledge. Edmund saw the drop for a second in mid-air, shining like a diamond. But the moment it touched the snow there was a hissing sound and there stood a jewelled cup full of something that steamed. The dwarf immediately took this and handed it to Edmund with a bow and a smile; not a very nice smile. Edmund felt much better as he began to sip the hot drink. It was something he had never tasted before, very sweet and foamy and creamy, and it warmed him right down to his toes.

'It is dull, Son of Adam, to drink without eating,' said the Queen presently. 'What would you like best to eat?'

'Turkish Delight, please, Your Majesty,' said Edmund. The Queen let another drop fall from her bottle on to the snow, and instantly there appeared a round box, tied with green silk ribbon, which, when opened, turned out to contain several pounds of the best Turkish Delight. Each piece was sweet and light to the very centre and Edmund had never tasted anything more delicious. He was quite warm now, and very comfortable.

While he was eating the Queen kept asking him questions. At first Edmund tried to remember that it is rude to speak with one's mouth full, but soon he forgot about this and thought only of trying to shovel down as much Turkish Delight as he could, and the more he ate the more he wanted to eat, and he never asked himself why the Queen should be so inquisitive. She got him to tell her that he had one brother and two sisters, and that one of his sisters had already been in Narnia and had met a Faun there, and that no one except himself and his brother and his sisters knew anything about Narnia. She seemed especially interested in the fact that there were

four of them, and kept on coming back to it. 'You are sure there are just four of you?' she asked. 'Two Sons of Adam and two Daughters of Eve, neither more nor less?' and Edmund, with his mouth full of Turkish Delight, kept on saying, 'Yes, I told you that before,' and forgetting to call her 'Your Majesty', but she didn't seem to mind now.

At last the Turkish Delight was all finished and Edmund was looking very hard at the empty box and wishing that she would ask him whether he would like some more. Probably the Queen knew quite well what he was thinking; for she knew, though Edmund did not, that this was enchanted Turkish Delight and that anyone who had once tasted it would want more and more of it, and would even, if they were allowed, go on eating it till they killed themselves. But she did not offer him any more. Instead, she said to him,

'Son of Adam, I should so much like to see your brother and your two sisters. Will you bring them to see me?'

'I'll try,' said Edmund, still looking at the empty box.

'Because, if you did come again – bringing them with you of course – I'd be able to give you some more Turkish Delight. I can't do it now, the magic will only work once. In my own house it would be another matter.'

'Why can't we go to your house now?' said Edmund. When he had first got on the sledge he had been afraid that she might drive away with him to some unknown place from which he would not be able to get back; but he had forgotten about that fear now.

'It is a lovely place, my house,' said the Queen. 'I am sure you would like it. There are whole rooms full of Turkish Delight, and what's more, I have no children of my own. I want a nice boy whom I could bring up as a Prince and who would be King of Narnia when I am gone. While he was Prince he would wear a gold crown and eat Turkish Delight all day long; and you are much the cleverest and handsomest young man I've ever met. I think I would like to make you the Prince – some day, when you bring the others to visit me.'

'Why not now?' said Edmund. His face had become very red and his mouth and fingers were sticky. He did not look either clever or handsome, whatever the Queen might say.

'Oh, but if I took you there now,' said she, 'I shouldn't see your brother and your sisters. I very much want to know your charming relations. You are to be the Prince and – later on – the King; that is understood. But you must have courtiers and nobles. I will make your brother a Duke and your sisters Duchesses.'

'There's nothing special about *them*,' said Edmund, 'and, anyway, I could always bring them some other time.'

'Ah, but once you were in my house,' said the Queen, 'you might forget all about them. You would be enjoying yourself so much that you wouldn't want the bother of going to fetch them. No. You must go back to your own country now and come to me another day, *with them*, you understand. It is no good coming without them.'

'But I don't even know the way back to my own country,' pleaded Edmund.

'That's easy,' answered the Queen. 'Do you see that lamp?' She pointed with her wand and Edmund turned and saw the same lamp-post under which Lucy had met the Faun. 'Straight on, beyond that, is the way to the World of Men. And now look the other way' – here she pointed in the opposite direction – 'and tell me if you can see two little hills rising above the trees.'

'I think I can,' said Edmund.

'Well, my house is between those two hills. So next time you come you have only to find the lamp-post and look for those two hills and walk through the wood till you reach my house. But remember – you must bring the others with you. I might have to be very angry with you if you came alone.'

'I'll do my best,' said Edmund.

'And, by the way,' said the Queen, 'you needn't tell them about me. It would be fun to keep it a secret between us two, wouldn't it? Make it a surprise for them. Just bring them along to the two hills – a clever boy like you will easily think of some excuse for doing that – and when you come to my house you could just say, "Let's see who lives here" or something like that. I am sure that would be best.

If your sister has met one of the Fauns, she may have heard strange
stories about me – nasty stories that might make her afraid to come
to me. Fauns will say anything, you know, and now –'

'Please, please,' said Edmund suddenly, 'please couldn't I have just
one piece of Turkish Delight to eat on the way home?'

'No, no,' said the Queen with a laugh, 'you must wait till next
time.' While she spoke, she signalled to the dwarf to drive on, but as
the sledge swept away out of sight, the Queen waved to Edmund,
calling out, 'Next time! Next time! Don't forget. Come soon.'

Edmund was still staring after the sledge when he heard someone
calling his own name, and looking round he saw Lucy coming
towards him from another part of the wood.

'Oh, Edmund!' she cried. 'So you've got in too! Isn't it wonderful
and now –'

'All right,' said Edmund,
'I see you were right and it
is a magic wardrobe after
all. I'll say I'm sorry if
you like. But where on
earth have you been all
this time? I've been looking
for you everywhere.'

'If I'd known you had got in
I'd have waited for you,' said Lucy, who was too happy and excited
to notice how snappishly Edmund spoke or how flushed and strange
his face was. 'I've been having lunch with dear Mr Tumnus, the Faun,
and he's very well and the White Witch has done nothing to him for
letting me go, so he thinks she can't have found out and perhaps

everything is going to be all right after all.'

'The White Witch?' said Edmund. 'Who's she?'

'She is a perfectly terrible person,' said Lucy. 'She calls herself the Queen of Narnia though she has no right to be queen at all, and all the Fauns and Dryads and Naiads and Dwarfs and Animals – at least all the good ones – simply hate her. And she can turn people into stone and do all kinds of horrible things. And she has made a magic so that it is always winter in Narnia – always winter, but it never gets to Christmas. And she drives about on a sledge, drawn by reindeer, with her wand in her hand and a crown on her head.'

Edmund was already feeling uncomfortable from having eaten too many sweets, and when he heard that the Lady he had made friends with was a dangerous witch he felt even more uncomfortable. But he still wanted to taste that Turkish Delight again more than he wanted anything else.

'Who told you all that stuff about the White Witch?' he asked.

'Mr Tumnus, the Faun,' said Lucy.

'You can't always believe what Fauns say,' said Edmund, trying to sound as if he knew far more about them than Lucy.

'Who said so?' asked Lucy.

'Everyone knows it,' said Edmund; 'ask anybody you like. But it's pretty poor sport standing here in the snow. Let's go home.'

'Yes, let's,' said Lucy. 'Oh, Edmund, I *am* glad you've got in too. The others will have to believe in Narnia now that both of us have been there. What fun it will be!'

But Edmund secretly thought that it would not be as good fun for him as for her. He would have to admit that Lucy had been right, before all the others, and he felt sure the others would all be on the side of the Fauns and the animals; but he was already more than half on the side of the Witch. He did not know what he would say, or how he would keep his secret, once they were all talking about Narnia.

By this time they had walked a good way. Then suddenly they felt coats around them instead of branches and next moment they were both standing outside the wardrobe in the empty room.

'I say,' said Lucy, 'you do look awful, Edmund. Don't you feel well?'

'I'm all right,' said Edmund, but this was not true. He was feeling very sick.

'Come on then,' said Lucy, 'let's find the others. What a lot we shall have to tell them! And what wonderful adventures we shall have now that we're all in it together.'

Dick King-Smith

THE HODGEHEG

ILLUSTRATED BY MIKE TERRY

THE MAGIC CROSSING

Max the hedgehog is trying to discover a safe way for hedgehogs to cross the road. In doing so he bangs his head, and now everything he says comes out backwards. But Max is undaunted.

THAT evening Max waited until he was sure that Pa was out of the way, in the garden of Number 5B. The people in 5A always put out bread-and-milk for Max's family, but the people in 5B often provided something much better for their hedgehogs – tinned dog-food.

Every evening Pa crept through the dividing hedge to see if he could nick a saucerful of Munchimeat before his neighbour woke from the day's sleep.

'Ma,' said Max, 'I'm walking for a go.'

Ma was quick at translating by now.

'Did Pa say you could go?' she said.

'No,' said Max, 'but he couldn't say I didn't,' and before Ma could do anything he trotted off along the garden path.

'Oh, Max!' called Ma. 'Are you sure you'll be all right?'

'Yes, of course,' said Max. 'I'll be quite KO.'

Once outside the garden gate he turned left and set off up the road, in the opposite direction to his previous effort. By now he was used to the noise and the brightness, and confident that he was safe from traffic as long as he did not step down into the road. When a human passed, he stood still. The creatures did not notice you, he found, if you did not move.

He trotted on, past the garden of Number 9A with its widow and six kids, until the row of houses ended and a high factory wall began, so high that he would not have been able to read the notice on it beside the factory entrance: Max Speed 5 M.P.H. it said.

Max kept going (a good deal more slowly than this), and then suddenly, once again, he saw not far ahead what he was seeking. Again, there were people crossing the street!

This time they did not go in ones and twos at random, but waited all together and then, at some signal he supposed, crossed at the same time. Max drew nearer, until he could hear at intervals a high rapid peep-peep-peeping noise, at the sound of which the traffic stopped and the people walked over in safety.

Creeping closer still, tight up against the wall, he finally reached the crossing-place, and now he could see this new magic method. The bunch of humans stood and watched, just above their heads, a picture of a little red man standing quite still. The people stood quite still. Then suddenly the little red man disappeared and underneath him there was a picture of a little green man, walking, swinging his

arms. The people walked, swinging their arms, while the high, rapid peep-peep-peeping noise warned the traffic not to move.

Max sat and watched for quite a long time, fascinated by the red man and the green man. He rather wished they could have been a red hedgehog and a green hedgehog, but that was not really important, as long as hedgehogs could cross here safely. That was all he had to prove, and the sooner the better.

He edged forward, until he was just behind the waiting humans, and watched tensely for the little green man to walk.

What Max had not bargained for, when the bunch of people moved off at the peep-peep-peeping of the little green man, was that another bunch would be coming towards him from the other side of the street. So that when he was about half-way across, hurrying along at the heels of one crowd, he was suddenly confronted by another. He dodged about in a forest of legs, in great danger of being

stepped on. No one seemed to notice his small shape and indeed he was kicked by a large foot and rolled backwards.

Picking himself up, he looked across and found to his horror that the green man was gone and the red man had reappeared. Frantically Max ran on as the traffic began to move, and reached the far side inches in front of a great wheel that almost brushed his backside. The shock of so narrow an escape made him roll up, and for some time he lay in the gutter whilst above his head the humans stepped on to or off the pavement and the noisy green man and the silent red man lit up in turn.

After a while there seemed to be fewer people about, and Max uncurled and climbed over the kerb. He turned right and set off in the direction of home. How to recross the street was something he had not yet worked out, but in his experience neither striped bits nor red and green men were the answer.

As usual he kept close to the wall at the inner edge of the pavement, a wall that presently gave place to iron railings. These were wide enough apart for even the largest hedgehog to pass between. Max slipped through. In the light of a full moon he could see before him a wide stretch of grass and he ran across it until the noise and stink of the traffic were left behind.

'Am I where?' said Max, looking round him. His nose told him of the scent of flowers (in the Ornamental Gardens), his eyes told him of a strange-shaped building (the Bandstand), and his ears told him of the sound of splashing water (as the fountain spouted endlessly in the Lily-Pond).

Of course! This was the place that Pa had told them all about! This was the Park!

'Hip, hip, roohay!' cried Max to the moon, and away he ran.

For the next few hours he trotted busily about the Park, shoving his snout into everything. Like most children, he was not only nosy but noisy too, and at the sound of his coming the mice scuttled under the Bandstand, the snakes slid away through the Ornamental Gardens, and the frogs plopped into the safe depths of the Lily-Pond. Max caught nothing.

At last he began to feel rather tired and to think how nice it would be to go home to bed. But which way was home?

Max considered this, and came to the unhappy conclusion that he was lost. Just then he saw, not far away, a hedgehog crossing the path, a large hedgehog, a Pa-sized hedgehog! What luck! Pa had crossed the street to find him! He ran forward, but when he reached the animal he found it was a complete stranger.

'Oh,' said Max, 'I peg your bardon. I thought you were a different hodgeheg.'

The stranger looked curiously at him. 'Are you feeling all right?' he said.

'Yes, thanks,' said Max. 'Trouble is, I go to want home. But I won't know the day.'

'You mean . . . you don't know the way?'

'Yes.'

'Well, where do you live?' asked the strange hedgehog.

'Number 5A.'

'Indeed? Well now, listen carefully, young fellow. Go up this path – it will take you back to the street – and a little way along you'll see a strange sort of house that humans use. It's a tall house, just big enough for one human to stand up in, and it has windows on three

sides and it's bright red. If you cross there, you'll fetch up right by your own front gate. OK?'

'KO,' said Max, 'and thanks.'

As soon as he was through the Park railings, he saw the tall red house. He trotted up close to it. It was lit up, and sure enough there was a human inside it. He was holding something to his ear and Max could see that his lips were moving. How odd, thought Max, moving very close now, he's standing in there talking to himself!

At that instant the man put down the receiver and pushed open the door of the tele-phone booth, a door designed to clear the pavement by about an inch, the perfect height for giving an inquisitive young hedgehog — for the second time in his short life — a tremendous bang on the head.

Lewis Carroll

ALICE IN WONDERLAND

ILLUSTRATED BY IAN BECK

THE QUEEN'S CROQUET-GROUND

Alice has followed the White Rabbit down a rabbit-hole and finds herself in Wonderland, where anything can happen.

A LARGE rose-tree stood near the entrance of the garden: the roses growing on it were white, but there were three gardeners at it, busily painting them red. Alice thought this a very curious thing, and she went nearer to watch them, and just as she came up to them she heard one of them say, 'Look out now, Five! Don't go splashing paint over me like that!'

'I couldn't help it,' said Five in a sulky tone. 'Seven jogged my elbow.'

On which Seven looked up and said, 'That's right, Five! Always lay the blame on others!'

'*You'd* better not talk!' said Five. 'I heard the Queen say only yesterday you deserved to be beheaded!'

'What for?' said the one who had spoken first.

'That's none of *your* business, Two!' said Seven.

'Yes it *is* his business!' said Five, 'and I'll tell him — it was for bringing the cook tulip-roots instead of onions.'

Seven flung down his brush, and had just begun, 'Well, of all the unjust things —' when his eye chanced to fall upon Alice, as she stood watching them, and he checked himself suddenly: the others looked round also, and all of them bowed low.

'Would you tell me,' said Alice, a little timidly, 'why you are painting those roses?'

Five and Seven said nothing, but looked at Two. Two began in a low voice, 'Why the fact is, you see, Miss, this here ought to have been a *red* rose-tree, and we put a white one in by mistake; and if the Queen was to find out, we should all have our heads cut off, you know. So you see, Miss, we're doing our best afore she comes, to —' At this moment Five, who had been anxiously looking across the garden, called out, 'The Queen! The Queen!' and the three gardeners instantly threw themselves flat upon their faces. There was a sound of many footsteps, and Alice looked round, eager to see the Queen.

First came ten soldiers carrying clubs; these were all shaped like the three gardeners, oblong and flat, with their hands and feet at the corners: next the ten courtiers; these were ornamented all over with diamonds, and walked two and two, as the soldiers did. After these came the royal children; there were ten of them, and the little dears came jumping merrily along hand in hand, in couples; they were all ornamented with hearts. Next came the guests, mostly Kings and Queens, and among them Alice recognized the White Rabbit: it was talking in a hurried nervous manner, smiling at everything that was

said, and went by without noticing her. Then followed the Knave of Hearts, carrying the King's crown on a crimson velvet cushion; and, last of all this grand procession, came THE KING AND QUEEN OF HEARTS.

Alice was rather doubtful whether she ought not to lie down on her face like the three gardeners, but she could not remember ever having heard of such a rule at processions; 'and besides, what would be the use of a procession,' thought she, 'if people had all to lie down upon their faces, so that they couldn't see it?' So she stood still where she was, and waited.

When the procession came opposite to Alice, they all stopped and looked at her, and the Queen said severely, 'Who is this?' She said it to the Knave of Hearts, who only bowed and smiled in reply.

'Idiot!' said the Queen, tossing her head impatiently; and, turning to Alice, she went on, 'What's your name, child?'

'My name is Alice, so please Your Majesty,' said Alice very politely; but she added, to herself, 'Why, they're only a pack of cards, after all. I needn't be afraid of them!'

'And who are *these*?' said the Queen, pointing to the three gardeners who were lying round the rose-tree; for, you see, as they were lying on their faces, and the pattern on their backs was the same as the rest of the pack, she could not tell whether they were gardeners, or soldiers, or courtiers, or three of her own children.

'How should *I* know?' said Alice, surprised at her own courage. 'It's no business of *mine*.'

The Queen turned crimson with fury, and, after glaring at her for

a moment like a wild beast, screamed, 'Off with her head! Off —'

'Nonsense!' said Alice, very loudly and decidedly, and the Queen was silent.

The King laid his hand upon her arm, and timidly said, 'Consider, my dear: she is only a child!'

The Queen turned angrily away from him, and said to the Knave, 'Turn them over!'

The Knave did so, very carefully, with one foot.

'Get up!' said the Queen, in a shrill, loud voice, and the three gardeners instantly jumped up, and began bowing to the King, the Queen, the royal children, and everybody else.

'Leave off that!' screamed the Queen. 'You make me giddy.' And then, turning to the rose-tree, she went on, 'What *have* you been doing here?'

'May it please Your Majesty,' said Two, in a very humble tone, going down on one knee as he spoke, 'we were trying –'

'*I* see!' said the Queen, who had meanwhile been examining the roses. 'Off with their heads!' and the procession moved on, three of the soldiers remaining behind to execute the unfortunate gardeners, who ran to Alice for protection.

'You shan't be beheaded!' said Alice, and she put them into a large flower-pot that stood near. The three soldiers wandered about for a minute or two, looking for them, and then quietly marched off after the others.

'Are their heads off?' shouted the Queen.

'Their heads are gone, if it please Your Majesty!' the soldiers shouted in reply.

'That's right!' shouted the Queen. 'Can you play croquet?'

The soldiers were silent, and looked at Alice, as the question was evidently meant for her.

'Yes!' shouted Alice.

'Come on, then!' roared the Queen, and Alice joined the procession, wondering very much what would happen next.

'It's — it's a very fine day!' said a timid voice at her side. She was walking by the White Rabbit, who was peeping anxiously into her face.

'Very,' said Alice: '— where's the Duchess?'

'Hush! Hush!' said the Rabbit in a low, hurried tone. He looked anxiously over his shoulder as he spoke, and then raised himself upon tiptoe, put his mouth close to her ear, and whispered, 'She's under sentence of execution.'

'What for?' said Alice.

'Did you say "What a pity!"?' the Rabbit asked.

'No, I didn't,' said Alice. 'I don't think it's at all a pity. I said, "What for?"'

'She boxed the Queen's ears —' the Rabbit began. Alice gave a little scream of laughter. 'Oh, hush!' the Rabbit whispered in a frightened tone. 'The Queen will hear you! You see, she came rather late, and the Queen said —'

'Get to your places!' shouted the Queen in a voice of thunder, and people began running about in all directions, tumbling up against each other; however, they got settled down in a minute or two, and the game began. Alice thought she had never seen such a curious croquet-ground in all her life; it was all ridges and furrows; the balls were live hedgehogs, the mallets live flamingoes, and the soldiers had to double themselves up and stand on their hands and feet, to make the arches.

The chief difficulty Alice found at first was in managing her flamingo: she succeeded in getting its body tucked away, comfortably enough, under her arm, with its legs hanging down, but generally, just as she had got its neck nicely straightened out, and was going to give the hedgehog a blow with its head, it *would* twist itself round and look up in her face, with such a puzzled expression that she could not help bursting out laughing: and when she had got its head down, and was going to begin again, it was very provoking to find that the hedgehog had unrolled itself, and was in the act of crawling away: besides all this, there was generally a ridge or furrow in the way wherever she wanted to send the hedgehog to, and, as the doubled-up soldiers were always getting up and walking off to other parts of the ground, Alice soon came to the conclusion that it was a very difficult game indeed.

The players all played at once without waiting for turns, quarrelling all the while, and fighting for the hedgehogs; and in a very short time the Queen was in a furious passion, and went stamping about, and shouting, 'Off with his head!' or, 'Off with her head!' about once a minute.

Roald Dahl

SPOTTY POWDER

ILLUSTRATED BY QUENTIN BLAKE

This is one of several chapters that were originally included in
Charlie and the Chocolate Factory. *But there were too many
naughty children in the earlier versions of the book, so one by one,
these chapters had to be dropped.*

'THIS stuff,' said Mr Wonka, 'is going to cause chaos in schools all over the world when I get it in the shops.'

The room they now entered had rows and rows of pipes coming straight up out of the floor. The pipes were bent over at the top and they looked like large walking-sticks. Out of every pipe there trickled a stream of white crystals. Hundreds of Oompa-Loompas were running to and fro, catching the crystals in little golden boxes and stacking the boxes against the walls.

'Spotty Powder!' exclaimed Mr Wonka, beaming at the company. 'There it is! That's it! Fantastic stuff!'

'It looks like sugar,' said Miranda Piker.

'It's *meant* to look like sugar,' Mr Wonka said. 'And it *tastes* like sugar. But it *isn't* sugar. Oh, dear me, no.'

'Then what is it?' asked Miranda Piker, speaking rather rudely.

'That door over there,' said Mr Wonka, turning away from Miranda and pointing to a small red door at the far end of the room, 'leads directly down to the machine that makes the powder. Twice a day, I go down there myself to feed it. But I'm the only one. Nobody ever comes with me.'

They all stared at the little door on which it said MOST SECRET – KEEP OUT.

The hum and throb of powerful machinery could be heard coming up from the depths below, and the floor itself was vibrating all the time. The children could feel it through the soles of their shoes.

Miranda Piker now pushed forward and stood in front of Mr Wonka. She was a nasty-looking girl with a smug face and a smirk on her mouth, and whenever she spoke it was always with a voice that seemed to be saying, 'Everybody is a fool except me.'

'OK,' Miranda Piker said, smirking at Mr Wonka. 'So what's the big news? What's this stuff meant to do when you eat it?'

'Ah-ha,' said Mr Wonka, his eyes sparkling with glee. 'You'd never guess that, not in a million years. Now listen. All you have to do is sprinkle it over your cereal at breakfast-time, pretending it's sugar. Then you eat it. And *then*, exactly five seconds after that, you come out in bright red spots all over your face and neck.'

'What sort of a silly ass wants spots on his face at breakfast-time?' said Miranda Piker.

'Let me finish,' said Mr Wonka. 'So then your mother looks at you across the table and says, "My poor child. You must have chickenpox. You can't possibly go to school today." So you stay at home. But by lunch-time, the spots have all disappeared.'

'Terrific!' shouted Charlie. 'That's just what I want for the day we have exams!'

'That is the ideal time to use it,' said Mr Wonka. 'But you mustn't do it too often or it'll give the game away. Keep it for the really nasty days.'

'Father!' cried Miranda Piker. 'Did you hear what this stuff does? It's shocking! It mustn't be allowed!'

Mr Piker, Miranda's father, stepped forward and faced Mr Wonka. He had a smooth white face like a boiled onion.

'Now see here, Wonka,' he said. 'I happen to be the headmaster of a large school, and I won't allow you to sell this rubbish to the

children! It's . . . it's criminal! Why, you'll ruin the school-system of the entire country!'

'I hope so,' said Mr Wonka.

'It's *got* to be stopped!' shouted Mr Piker, waving his cane.

'Who's going to stop it?' asked Mr Wonka. 'In *my* factory, I make things to please children. I don't care about grown-ups.'

'I am top of my form,' Miranda Piker said, smirking at Mr Wonka. 'And I've never missed a day's school in my life.'

'Then it's time you did,' Mr Wonka said.

'How dare you!' said Mr Piker.

'All holidays and vacations should be stopped!' cried Miranda. 'Children are meant to work, not play.'

'Quite right, my girl,' cried Mr Piker, patting Miranda on the top of the head. 'All work and no play has made you what you are today.'

'Isn't she wonderful?' said Mrs Piker, beaming at her daughter.

'Come on then, father!' cried Miranda. 'Let's go down into the cellar and smash the machine that makes this dreadful stuff!'

'Forward!' shouted Mr Piker, brandishing his cane and making a dash for the little red door on which it said MOST SECRET – KEEP OUT.

'Stop!' said Mr Wonka. 'Don't go in there! It's terribly secret!'

'Let's see you stop us, you old goat!' shouted Miranda.

'We'll smash it to smithereens!' yelled Mr Piker. And a few seconds later the two of them had disappeared through the door.

There was a moment's silence.

Then, far off in the distance, from somewhere deep underground, there came a fearful scream.

'That's my husband!' cried Mrs Piker, going blue in the face.

There was another scream.

'And that's Miranda!' yelled Mrs Piker, beginning to hop around in circles. 'What's happening to them? What have you got down there, you dreadful beast?'

'Oh, nothing much,' Mr Wonka answered. 'Just a lot of cogs and wheels and chains and things like that, all going round and round and round.'

'You villain!' she screamed. 'I know your tricks! You're grinding them into powder! In two minutes, my darling Miranda will come pouring out of one of those dreadful pipes, and so will my husband!'

'Of course,' said Mr Wonka. 'That's part of the recipe.'

'It's *what*!'

'We've got to use one or two schoolmasters occasionally or it wouldn't work.'

'Did you *hear* him?' shrieked Mrs Piker, turning to the others. 'He admits it! He's nothing but a cold-blooded murderer!'

Mr Wonka smiled and patted Mrs Piker gently on the arm. 'Dear lady,' he said, 'I was only joking.'

'Then why did they scream?' snapped Mrs Piker. 'I distinctly heard them scream!'

'Those weren't screams,' Mr Wonka said. 'They were laughs.'

'My husband never laughs,' said Mrs Piker.

Mr Wonka flicked his fingers, and up came an Oompa-Loompa.

'Kindly escort Mrs Piker to the boiler room,' Mr Wonka said. 'Don't fret, dear lady,' he went on, shaking Mrs Piker warmly by the hand. 'They'll all come out in the wash. There's nothing to worry about. Off you go. Thank you for coming. Farewell! Goodbye! A pleasure to meet you!'

'Listen, Charlie!' said Grandpa Joe. 'The Oompa-Loompas are starting to sing again!'

'Oh, Miranda Mary Piker!' sang the five Oompa-Loompas dancing about and laughing and beating madly on their tiny drums.

'*Oh, Miranda Mary Piker,*
How could anybody like her,
Such a priggish and revolting little kid.
So we said, "Why don't we fix her
In the Spotty-Powder mixer
Then we're bound to like her better than we did."
Soon this child who is so vicious
Will have gotten quite delicious,
And her classmates will have surely understood
That instead of saying, "Miranda!
Oh, the beast! We cannot stand her!"
They'll be saying, "Oh, how useful and how good!"'

~

Susan Coolidge

What Katy Did

ILLUSTRATED BY SHIRLEY HUGHES

The Day of Scrapes

Lively, quick-tempered Katy always means to be well-behaved, but somehow all her good intentions get forgotten or go horribly wrong!

MRS Knight's school, to which Katy and Clover and Cecy went, stood quite at the other end of the town from Dr Carr's. It was a low, one-storey building, and had a yard behind it, in which the girls played at recess. Unfortunately, next door to it was Miss Miller's school, equally large and popular, and with a yard behind it also. Only a high board fence separated the two playgrounds.

Mrs Knight was a stout, gentle woman, who moved slowly, and had a face which made you think of an amiable and well-disposed cow. Miss Miller, on the contrary, had black eyes, with black corkscrew curls waving about them, and was generally brisk and snappy. A constant feud raged between the two schools as to the respective merits of the teachers and the instruction. The Knight girls, for some unknown reason, considered themselves genteel and the Miller girls vulgar, and took no pains to conceal this opinion; while the Miller girls, on the other hand, retaliated by being as aggravating as they knew how. They spent their recesses and intermissions mostly in making faces through the knot-holes in the fence, and over the top of it, when they could get there, which wasn't an easy thing to do, as the fence was pretty high. The Knight girls could make faces too, for all their gentility. Their yard had one great advantage over the other: it possessed a wood-shed, with a climbable roof, which commanded Miss Miller's premises, and upon this the girls used to sit in rows, turning up their noses at the next yard, and irritating the foe by jeering remarks. 'Knights' and 'Millerites' the two schools called each other; and the feud raged so high that sometimes it was hardly safe for a Knight to meet a Millerite in the street; all of which, as may be imagined, was exceedingly improving both to the manners and morals of the young ladies concerned.

One morning, not long after the day in Paradise, Katy was late. She could not find her things. Her algebra, as she expressed it, had 'gone and lost itself', her slate was missing, and the string was off her sun-bonnet. She ran about, searching for these articles and banging doors, till Aunt Izzie was out of patience.

'As for your algebra,' she said, 'if it is that very dirty book with only one cover, and scribbled all over the leaves, you will find it under the kitchen table. Philly was playing before breakfast that it was a pig; no wonder, I'm sure, for it looks good for nothing else. How you do manage to spoil your school-books in this manner, Katy, I cannot imagine. It is less than a month since your father got you a new algebra, and look at it now – not fit to be carried about. I do wish you'd realize what books cost!

'About your slate,' she went on, 'I know nothing; but here is the bonnet-string;' taking it out of her pocket.

'Oh, thank you!' said Katy, hastily sticking it on with a pin.

'Katy Carr!' almost screamed Miss Izzie, 'what *are* you about? Pinning on your bonnet string! Mercy on me! What shiftless thing will you do next? Now stand still and don't fidget! You shan't stir till I have sewed it on properly.'

It wasn't easy to 'stand still and not fidget', with Aunt Izzie fussing away and lecturing, and now and then, in a moment of forgetfulness, sticking her needle into one's chin. Katy bore it as well as she could, only shifting perpetually from one foot to the other, and now and then uttering a little snort, like an impatient horse. The minute she was released she flew into the kitchen, seized the algebra, and rushed like a whirlwind to the gate, where good little Clover stood patiently waiting, though all ready herself, and terribly afraid she should be late.

'We shall have to run,' gasped Katy, quite out of breath. 'Aunt Izzie kept me. She has been so horrid!'

They did run as fast as they could, but time ran faster. And before they were half-way to school the town clock struck nine, and all the hope was over. This vexed Katy very much; for, though often late, she was always eager to be early.

'There,' she said, stopping short, 'I shall just tell Aunt Izzie that it was her fault. It is *too* bad.' And she marched into school in a very cross mood.

A day begun in this manner is pretty sure to end badly, as most of us know. All the morning through things seemed to go wrong. Katy missed twice in her grammar lesson, and lost her place in the class. Her hand shook so when she copied her composition, that the writing, not good at best, turned out almost illegible, so that Mrs Knight said it must be all done over again. This made Katy crosser than ever; and almost before she thought, she had whispered to Clover, 'How hateful!' And then, when just before recess all who had been speaking were requested to stand up, her conscience gave such

a twinge that she was forced to get up with the rest, and see a black mark put against her name on the list. The tears came into her eyes from vexation; and, for fear the other girls would notice them, she made a bolt for the yard as soon as the bell rang, and mounted up all alone to the wood-house roof, where she sat with her back to the school, fighting with her eyes, and trying to get her face in order before the rest should come.

Miss Miller's clock was about four minutes slower than Mrs Knight's, so the next playground was empty. It was a warm, breezy day, and as Katy sat there, suddenly a gust of wind came, and seizing her sun-bonnet, which was only half tied on, whirled it across the roof. She clutched after it as it flew, but too late. Once, twice, thrice it flapped, then it disappeared over the edge, and Katy, flying after, saw it lying in a crumpled lilac heap in the very middle of the enemy's yard.

This was horrible! Not merely losing the bonnet, for Katy was comfortably indifferent as to what became of her clothes, but to lose it so. In another minute the Miller girls would be out. Already she seemed to see them dancing war-dances round the unfortunate bonnet, pinning it on a pole, using it as a football, waving it over the fence, and otherwise treating it as Indians treat a captive taken in war. Was it to be endured? Never! Better die first! And with very much the feeling of a person who faces destruction rather than forfeit honour, Katy set her teeth, and, sliding rapidly down the roof, seized the fence, and with one bold leap vaulted into Miss Miller's yard.

Just then the recess bell tinkled; and a little Millerite who sat by the window, and who, for two seconds, had been dying to give the exciting information, squeaked out to the others: 'There's Katy Carr in our backyard!'

Out poured the Millerites, big and little. Their wrath and indignation at this daring invasion cannot be described. With a howl of fury they precipitated themselves upon Katy, but she was as quick as they, and holding the rescued bonnet in her hand, was already halfway up the fence.

There are moments when it is a fine thing to be tall. On this occasion Katy's long legs and arms served her an excellent turn. Nothing but a Daddy Longlegs ever climbed so fast or so wildly as she did now. In one second she had gained the top of the fence. Just as she went over a Millerite seized her by the last foot, and almost dragged her boot off.

Almost, not quite, thanks to the stout thread with which Aunt Izzie had sewed on the buttons. With a frantic kick Katy released herself, and had the satisfaction of seeing her assailant go head over heels backwards, while, with a shriek of triumph and fright, she herself plunged headlong into the midst of a group of Knights. They were listening with open mouths to the uproar, and now stood transfixed at the astonishing spectacle of one of their number absolutely returning alive from the camp of the enemy.

I cannot tell you what a commotion ensued. The Knights were beside themselves with pride and triumph. Katy was kissed and hugged, and made to tell her story over and over again, while rows of exulting girls sat on the wood-house roof to crow over the discomfited Millerites: and when, later, the foe rallied and began to retort over the fence, Clover, armed with a tack hammer, was lifted up in the arms of one of the tall girls to rap the intruding knuckles as they appeared on the top. This she did with such goodwill that the Millerites were glad to drop down again, and mutter vengeance at a safe distance. Altogether it was a great day for the school, a day to be remembered. As time went on, Katy, what with the excitement of her adventure and of being praised and petted by the big girls, grew perfectly reckless, and hardly knew what she said or did.

A. A. Milne

WINNIE-THE-POOH

ILLUSTRATED BY E. H. SHEPARD

POOH AND PIGLET GO HUNTING AND NEARLY CATCH A WOOZLE

THE Piglet lived in a very grand house in the middle of a beech-tree, and the beech-tree was in the middle of the Forest, and the Piglet lived in the middle of the house. Next to his house was a piece of broken board which had: 'TRESPASSERS W' on it. When Christopher Robin asked the Piglet what it meant, he said it was his grandfather's name, and had been in the family for a long time. Christopher Robin said you *couldn't* be called Trespassers W, and Piglet said yes, you could, because his grandfather was, and it was short for Trespassers Will, which was short for Trespassers William. And his grandfather had had two names in case he lost one – Trespassers after an uncle, and William after Trespassers.

'I've got two names,' said Christopher Robin carelessly.

'Well, there you are, that proves it,' said Piglet.

One fine winter's day when Piglet was brushing away the snow

110

in front of his house, he happened to look up, and there was Winnie-the-Pooh. Pooh was walking round and round in a circle, thinking of something else, and when Piglet called to him, he just went on walking.

'Hallo!' said Piglet, 'what are *you* doing?'

'Hunting,' said Pooh.

'Hunting what?'

'Tracking something,' said Winnie-the-Pooh very mysteriously.

'Tracking what?' said Piglet, coming closer.

'That's just what I ask myself. I ask myself, What?'

'What do you think you'll answer?'

'I shall have to wait until I catch up with it,' said Winnie-the-Pooh. 'Now, look there.' He pointed to the ground in front of him. 'What do you see there?'

'Tracks,' said Piglet. 'Paw-marks.' He gave a little squeak of excitement. 'Oh, Pooh! Do you think it's a – a – a Woozle?'

'It may be,' said Pooh. 'Sometimes it is, and sometimes it isn't. You can never tell with paw-marks.'

With these few words he went on tracking, and Piglet, after watching him for a minute or two, ran after him. Winnie-the-Pooh had come to a sudden stop, and was bending over the tracks in a puzzled sort of way.

'What's the matter?' asked Piglet.

'It's a very funny thing,' said Bear, 'but there seem to be two animals now. This – whatever-it-was – has been joined by another –

whatever-it-is — and the two of them are now proceeding in company. Would you mind coming with me, Piglet, in case they turn out to be Hostile Animals?'

Piglet scratched his ear in a nice sort of way, and said that he had nothing to do until Friday, and would be delighted to come, in case it really was a Woozle.

'You mean, in case it really is two Woozles,' said Winnie-the-Pooh, and Piglet said that anyhow he had nothing to do until Friday. So off they went together.

There was a small spinney of larch-trees just here, and it seemed as if the two Woozles, if that is what they were, had been going round this spinney; so round this spinney went Pooh and Piglet after them; Piglet passing the time by telling Pooh what his Grandfather Trespassers W had done to Remove Stiffness after tracking, and how his Grandfather Trespassers W had suffered in his later years from Shortness of Breath, and other matters of interest, and Pooh wondering what a Grandfather was like, and if perhaps this was Two Grandfathers they were after now, and, if so, whether he would be allowed to take one home and keep it, and what Christopher Robin would say. And still the tracks went on in front of them . . .

Suddenly Winnie-the-Pooh stopped, and pointed excitedly in front of him. '*Look!*'

'What?' said Piglet, with a jump. And then, to show that he hadn't been frightened, he jumped up and down once or twice more in an exercising sort of way.

'The tracks!' said Pooh. '*A third animal has joined the other two!*'

'Pooh!' cried Piglet. 'Do you think it is another Woozle?'

'No,' said Pooh, 'because it makes different marks. It is either Two Woozles and one, as it might be, Wizzle, or Two, as it might be, Wizzles and one, if so it is, Woozle. Let us continue to follow them.'

So they went on, feeling just a little anxious now, in case the three animals in front of them were of Hostile Intent. And Piglet wished very much that his Grandfather T.W. were there, instead of elsewhere, and Pooh thought how nice it would be if they met Christopher Robin suddenly but quite accidentally, and only because he liked Christopher Robin so much. And then, all of a sudden, Winnie-the-Pooh stopped again, and licked the tip of his nose in a cooling manner, for he was feeling more hot and anxious than ever in his life before. *There were four animals in front of them!*

'Do you see, Piglet? Look at their tracks! Three, as it were, Woozles, and one, as it was, Wizzle. *Another Woozle has joined them!*'

And so it seemed to be. There were the tracks; crossing over each other here, getting muddled up with each other there; but, quite plainly every now and then, the tracks of four sets of paws.

'I *think*,' said Piglet, when he had licked the tip of his nose too, and found that it brought very little comfort, 'I *think* that I have just remembered something. I have just remembered something that I forgot to do yesterday and shan't be able to do tomorrow. So I suppose I really ought to go back and do it now.'

'We'll do it this afternoon, and

I'll come with you,' said Pooh.

'It isn't the sort of thing you can do in the afternoon,' said Piglet quickly. 'It's a very particular morning thing, that has to be done in the morning, and, if possible, between the hours of – What would you say the time was?'

'About twelve,' said Winnie-the-Pooh, looking at the sun.

'Between, as I was saying, the hours of twelve and twelve five. So, really, dear old Pooh, if you'll excuse me – *What's that?*'

Pooh looked up at the sky, and then, as he heard the whistle again, he looked up into the branches of a big oak-tree, and then he saw a friend of his.

'It's Christopher Robin,' he said.

'Ah, then you'll be all right,' said Piglet. 'You'll be quite safe with *him*. Good-bye,' and he trotted off home as quickly as he could, very glad to be Out of All Danger again.

Christopher Robin came slowly down his tree.

'Silly old Bear,' he said, 'what *were* you doing? First you went round the spinney twice by yourself, and then Piglet ran after you and you went round again together, and then you were just going round a fourth time –'

'Wait a moment,' said Winnie-the-Pooh, holding up his paw.

He sat down and thought, in the most thoughtful way he could think. Then he fitted his paw into one of the Tracks . . . and then he scratched his nose twice, and stood up.

'Yes,' said Winnie-the-Pooh.

'I see now,' said Winnie-the-Pooh.

'I have been Foolish and Deluded,' said he, 'and I am a Bear of No Brain at All.'

'You're the Best Bear in All the World,' said Christopher Robin soothingly.

'Am I?' said Pooh hopefully. And then he brightened up suddenly.

'Anyhow,' he said, 'it is nearly Luncheon Time.'

So he went home for it.

Oscar Wilde

THE HAPPY PRINCE

ILLUSTRATED BY PAULINE BAYNES

H IGH above the city, on a tall column, stood the statue of the Happy Prince. He was gilded all over with thin leaves of fine gold, for eyes he had two bright sapphires, and a large red ruby glowed on his sword-hilt.

He was very much admired indeed. 'He is as beautiful as a weathercock,' remarked one of the Town Councillors who wished to gain a reputation for having artistic tastes; 'only not quite so useful,' he added, fearing lest people should think him unpractical, which he really was not.

'Why can't you be like the Happy Prince?' asked a sensible mother of her little boy who was crying for the moon. 'The Happy Prince never dreams of crying for anything.'

'I am glad there is someone in the world who is quite happy,' muttered a disappointed man as he gazed at the wonderful statue.

'He looks just like an angel,' said the Charity Children as they came out of the cathedral in their bright scarlet cloaks and their clean white pinafores.

'How do you know?' said the Mathematical Master.

'You have never seen one.'

'Ah! But we have, in our dreams,' answered the children; and the Mathematical Master frowned and looked very severe, for he did not approve of children dreaming.

One night there flew over the city a little Swallow. His friends had gone away to Egypt six weeks before, but he had stayed behind, for he was in love with the most beautiful Reed. He had met her early in the spring as he was flying down the river after a big yellow moth, and had been so attracted by her slender waist that he had stopped to talk to her.

'Shall I love you?' said the Swallow, who liked to come to the point at once, and the Reed made him a low bow. So he flew round and round her, touching the water with his wings, and making silver ripples. This was his courtship, and it lasted all through the summer.

'It is a ridiculous attachment,' twittered the other Swallows; 'she has no money, and far too many relations'; and indeed the river was quite full of Reeds. Then, when the autumn came they all flew away.

After they had gone he felt lonely, and began to tire of his lady-love. 'She has no conversation,' he said, 'and I am afraid that she is a coquette, for she is always flirting with the wind.' And certainly, whenever the wind blew, the Reed made the most graceful curtsies. 'I admit that she is domestic,' he continued, 'but I love travelling, and my wife, consequently, should love travelling also.'

'Will you come away with me?' he said finally to her, but the Reed shook her head, she was so attached to her home.

'You have been trifling with me,' he cried. 'I am off to the Pyramids. Good-bye!' and he flew away.

All day long he flew, and at night-time he arrived at the city. 'Where shall I put up?' he said; 'I hope the town has made preparations.'

Then he saw the statue on the tall column.

'I will put up there,' he cried; 'it is a fine position, with plenty of fresh air.' So he alighted just between the feet of the Happy Prince.

'I have a golden bedroom,' he said softly to himself as he looked round, and he prepared to go to sleep; but just as he was putting his head under his wing a large drop of water fell on him. 'What a curious thing!' he cried. 'There is not a single cloud in the sky, the stars are quite clear and bright, and yet it is raining. The climate in the north of Europe is really dreadful. The Reed used to like the rain, but that was merely her selfishness.'

Then another drop fell.

'What is the use of a statue if it cannot keep the rain off?' he said; 'I must look for a good chimney-pot,' and he determined to fly away.

But before he had opened his wings, a third drop fell, and he looked up, and saw – Ah! What did he see?

The eyes of the Happy Prince were filled with tears, and tears were running down his golden cheeks. His face was so beautiful in the moonlight that the little swallow was filled with pity.

'Who are you?' he said.

'I am the Happy Prince.'

'Why are you weeping then?' asked the Swallow. 'You have quite drenched me.'

'When I was alive and had a human heart,' answered the statue, 'I did not know what tears were, for I lived in the Palace of Sans-Souci, where sorrow is not allowed to enter. In the daytime I played with my companions in the garden, and in the evening I led the dance in the Great Hall. Round the garden ran a very lofty wall, but I never cared to ask what lay beyond it, everything about me was so beautiful. My courtiers called me the Happy Prince, and happy indeed I was, if pleasure be happiness. So I lived, and so I died. And now that I am dead they have set me up here so high that I can see all the ugliness and all the misery of my city, and though my heart is made of lead yet I cannot choose but weep.'

'What! Is he not solid gold?' said the Swallow to himself. He was too polite to make any personal remarks out loud.

'Far away,' continued the statue in a low musical voice, 'far away in a little street there is a poor house. One of the windows is open, and through it I can see a woman seated at a table. Her face is thin and worn, and she has coarse, red hands, all pricked by the needle, for she is a seamstress. She is embroidering passion-flowers on a satin gown for the loveliest of the Queen's maids-of-honour to wear at the next Court ball. In a bed in the corner of the room her little boy is lying ill. He has a fever, and is asking for oranges. His mother has nothing to give him but river water, so he is crying. Swallow, Swallow, little Swallow, will

you not bring her the ruby out of my sword-hilt? My feet are fastened to this pedestal and I cannot move.'

'I am waited for in Egypt,' said the Swallow. 'My friends are flying up and down the Nile, and talking to the large lotus-flowers. Soon they will go to sleep in the tomb of the great King. The King is there himself in his painted coffin. He is wrapped in yellow linen, and embalmed with spices. Round his neck is a chain of pale green jade, and his hands are like withered leaves.'

'Swallow, Swallow, little Swallow,' said the Prince, 'will you not stay with me for one night and be my messenger? The boy is so thirsty, and the mother so sad.'

'I don't think I like boys,' answered the Swallow. 'Last summer, when I was staying on the river, there were two rude boys, the miller's sons, who were always throwing stones at me. They never hit me, of course; we swallows fly far too well for that, and besides I come of a family famous for its agility; but still, it was a mark of disrespect.'

But the Happy Prince looked so sad that the little Swallow was sorry. 'It is very cold here,' he said; 'but I will stay with you for one night, and be your messenger.'

So the Swallow picked out the great ruby from the Prince's sword, and flew away with it in his beak over the roofs of the town.

He passed by the cathedral tower, where the white marble angels were sculptured. He passed by the palace and heard the sound of dancing. A beautiful girl came out on the balcony with her lover. 'How wonderful the stars are,' he said to her, 'and how wonderful is the power of love!'

'I hope my dress will be ready in time for the State ball,' she answered; 'I have ordered passion-flowers to be embroidered on it: but the seamstresses are so lazy.'

He passed over the river, and saw the lanterns hanging to the masts of the ships. He passed over the Ghetto, and saw the old Jews bargaining with each other, and weighing out money in copper scales. At last he came to the poor house and looked in. The boy was tossing feverishly on his bed, and the mother had fallen asleep, she was so tired. In he hopped, and laid the great ruby on the table beside the woman's thimble. Then he flew gently round the bed, fanning the boy's forehead with his wings. 'How cool I feel!' said the boy, 'I must be getting better'; and he sank into a delicious slumber.

Then the Swallow flew back to the Happy Prince, and told him what he had done. 'It is curious,' he remarked, 'but I feel quite warm now, although it is so cold.'

'That is because you have done a good action,' said the Prince. And the little Swallow began to think, and then he fell asleep. Thinking always made him sleepy.

When day broke he flew down to the river and had a bath. 'What a remarkable phenomenon!' said the Professor of Ornithology as he was passing over the bridge. 'A swallow in winter!' And he wrote a long letter about it to the local newspaper. Everyone quoted it, it was full of so many words that they could not understand.

'Tonight I go to Egypt,' said the Swallow, and he was in high spirits at the prospect. He visited all the public monuments, and sat a long time on top of the church steeple. Wherever he went the Sparrows chirruped, and said to each other, 'What a distinguished stranger!' so he enjoyed himself very much.

When the moon rose he flew back to the Happy Prince. 'Have you any commissions for Egypt?' he cried. 'I am just starting.'

'Swallow, Swallow, little Swallow,' said the Prince, 'will you not stay with me one night longer?'

'I am waited for in Egypt,' answered the Swallow. 'Tomorrow my friends will fly up to the Second Cataract. The river-horse couches there among the bulrushes, and on a great granite throne sits the God Mennon. All night long he watches the stars, and when the morning star shines he utters one cry of joy, and then he is silent. At noon the yellow lions come down to the water's edge to drink. They have eyes like green beryls, and their roar is louder than the roar of the cataract.'

'Swallow, Swallow, little Swallow,' said the Prince, 'far away across the city I see a young man in a garret. He is leaning over a desk covered with papers, and in a tumbler by his side there is a bunch of withered violets. His hair is brown and crisp, and his lips are red as a pomegranate, and he has large and dreamy eyes. He is trying to finish a play for the Director of the Theatre, but he is too cold to write any more. There is no fire in the grate, and hunger has made him faint.'

'I will wait with you one night longer,' said the Swallow, who really had a good heart. 'Shall I take him another ruby?'

'Alas! I have no ruby now,' said the Prince: 'my eyes are all that I have left. They are made of rare sapphires, which were brought out of India a thousand years ago. Pluck out one of them and take it to him. He will sell it to the jeweller, and buy firewood, and finish his play.'

'Dear Prince,' said the Swallow, 'I cannot do that'; and he began to weep.

'Swallow, Swallow, little Swallow,' said the Prince, 'do as I command you.'

So the Swallow plucked out the Prince's eye, and flew away to the student's garret. It was easy enough to get in, as there was a hole in the roof. Through this he darted, and came into the room. The young man had his head buried in his hands, so he did not hear the flutter of the bird's wings, and when he looked up he found the beautiful sapphire lying on the withered violets.

'I am beginning to be appreciated,' he cried; 'this is from some great admirer. Now I can finish my play,' and he looked quite happy.

The next day the Swallow flew down to the harbour. He sat on the mast of a large vessel and watched the sailors hauling big chests out of the hold with ropes. 'Heave a-hoy!' they shouted as each chest came up. 'I am going to Egypt!' cried the Swallow, but nobody minded, and when the moon rose he flew back to the Happy Prince.

'I am come to bid you good-bye,' he cried.

'Swallow, Swallow, little Swallow,' said the Prince, 'will you not stay with me one night longer?'

'It is winter,' answered the Swallow, 'and the chill snow will soon be here. In Egypt the sun is warm on the green palm-trees, and the crocodiles lie in the mud and look lazily about them. My companions are building a nest in the Temple of Baalbek, and the pink and white doves are watching them, and cooing to each other. Dear Prince, I must leave you, but I will never forget you, and next spring I will bring you back two beautiful jewels in place of those you have given away. The ruby shall be redder than a red rose, and the sapphire shall be as blue as the great sea.'

'In the square below,' said the Happy Prince, 'there stands a little match-girl. She has let her matches fall in the gutter, and they are all spoiled. Her father will beat her if she does not bring home some money, and she is crying. She has no shoes or stockings, and her little head is bare. Pluck out my other eye, and

give it to her, and her father will not beat her.'

'I will stay with you one night longer,' said the Swallow, 'but I cannot pluck out your eye. You would be quite blind then.'

'Swallow, Swallow, little Swallow,' said the Prince, 'do as I command you.'

So he plucked out the Prince's other eye, and darted down with it. He swooped past the match-girl, and slipped the jewel into the palm of her hand. 'What a lovely bit of glass!' cried the little girl; and she ran home, laughing.

Then the Swallow came back to the Prince. 'You are blind now,' he said, 'so I will stay with you always.'

'No, little Swallow,' said the poor Prince, 'you must go away to Egypt.'

'I will stay with you always,' said the Swallow, and he slept at the Prince's feet.

All the next day he sat on the Prince's shoulder, and told him stories of what he had seen in strange lands. He told him of the red ibises, who stand in long rows on the banks of the Nile, and catch goldfish in their beaks; of the Sphinx, who is as old as the world itself, and lives in the desert, and knows everything; of the merchants, who walk slowly by the side of their camels and carry amber beads in their hands; of the King of the Mountains of the Moon, who is as black as ebony, and worships a large crystal; of the great green snake that sleeps in a palm-tree, and has twenty priests to feed it with honey-cakes; and of the pygmies who sail over a big lake on large flat leaves, and are always at war with the butterflies.

'Dear little Swallow,' said the Prince, 'you tell me of marvellous things, but more marvellous than anything is the suffering of men and of women. There is no Mystery so great as Misery. Fly over my city, little Swallow, and tell me what you see there.'

So the Swallow flew over the great city, and saw the rich making merry in their beautiful houses, while the beggars were sitting at the gates. He flew into dark lanes, and saw the white faces of starving children looking out listlessly at the black

streets. Under the archway of a bridge two little boys were lying in one another's arms to try and keep themselves warm. 'How hungry we are!' they said. 'You must not lie here,' shouted the watchman, and they wandered out into the rain.

Then he flew back and told the Prince what he had seen.

'I am covered with fine gold,' said the Prince, 'you must take it off, leaf by leaf, and give it to my poor; the living always think that gold can make them happy.'

Leaf after leaf of the fine gold the Swallow picked off, till the Happy Prince looked quite dull and grey. Leaf after leaf of the fine gold he brought to the poor, and the children's faces grew

rosier, and they laughed and played games in the street. 'We have bread now!' they cried.

Then the snow came, and after the snow came the frost. The streets looked as if they were made of silver, they were so bright and glistening; long icicles like crystal daggers hung down from the eaves of the houses, everybody went about in furs, and the little boys wore scarlet caps and skated on the ice.

The poor little Swallow grew colder and colder, but he would not leave the Prince, he loved him too well. He picked up crumbs outside the baker's door when the baker was not looking, and tried to keep himself warm by flapping his wings.

But at last he knew that he was going to die. He had just enough strength to fly up to the Prince's shoulder once more. 'Good-bye, dear Prince!' he murmured. 'Will you let me kiss your hand?'

'I am glad that you are going to Egypt at last, little Swallow,' said the Prince, 'you have stayed too long here; but you must kiss me on the lips for I love you.'

'It is not to Egypt that I am going,' said the Swallow. 'I am going to the House of Death. Death is the brother of Sleep, is he not?'

And he kissed the Happy Prince on the lips, and fell down dead at his feet.

At that moment a curious crack sounded inside the statue, as if something had broken. The fact is that the leaden heart had snapped right in two. It certainly was a dreadfully hard frost.

Early the next morning the Mayor was walking in the square below in company with the Town Councillors. As they passed the column he looked up at the statue: 'Dear me! How shabby the Happy Prince looks!' he said.

'How shabby, indeed!' cried the Town Councillors, who always agreed with the Mayor: and they went up to look at it.

'The ruby has fallen out of his sword, his eyes are gone, and he is golden no longer,' said the Mayor; 'in fact, he is little better than a beggar!'

'Little better than a beggar,' said the Town Councillors.

'And here is actually a dead bird at his feet!' continued the Mayor. 'We must really issue a proclamation that birds are not to be allowed to die here.' And the Town Clerk made a note of

the suggestion.

So they pulled down the statue of the Happy Prince. 'As he is no longer beautiful he is no longer useful,' said the Art Professor at the University.

Then they melted the statue in a furnace, and the Mayor held a meeting of the Corporation to decide what was to be done with the metal. 'We must have another statue, of course,' he said, 'and it shall be a statue of myself.'

'Of myself,' said each of the Town Councillors, and they quarrelled. When I last heard of them they were quarrelling still.

'What a strange thing!' said the overseer of the workmen at the foundry. 'This broken lead heart will not melt in the furnace. We must throw it away.' So they threw it on a dust-heap where the dead Swallow was also lying.

'Bring me the two most precious things in the city,' said God to one of His Angels; and the Angel brought Him the leaden heart and the dead bird.

'You have rightly chosen,' said God, 'for in my garden of Paradise this little bird shall sing for evermore, and in my city of gold the Happy Prince shall praise me.'

Mrs Molesworth

THE CUCKOO CLOCK

ILLUSTRATED BY JUSTIN TODD

BUTTERFLY-LAND

*Griselda is staying with her two sweet but rather dull old aunts.
At first she is very bored, but then she discovers that the cuckoo clock is
magic and the cuckoo can take her to the most wonderful places.*

GRISELDA opened her eyes.

What did she see?

The loveliest, loveliest garden that ever or never a little girl's eyes saw. As for describing it, I cannot. I must leave a good deal to your fancy. It was just a *delicious* garden. There was a charming mixture of all that is needed to make a garden perfect – grass, velvety lawn rather; water, for a little brook ran tinkling in and out, playing bo-peep among the bushes; trees, of course, and flowers, of course, flowers of every shade and shape. But all these beautiful things Griselda did not at first give as much attention to as they deserved; her eyes were so occupied with a quite unusual sight that met them.

This was butterflies! Not that butterflies are so very uncommon, but butterflies, as Griselda saw them, I am quite sure, children, none of you ever saw, or are likely to see. There were such enormous numbers of them, and the variety of their colours and sizes was so great. They were fluttering about everywhere; the garden seemed actually alive with them.

Griselda stood for a moment in silent delight, feasting her eyes on the lovely things before her, enjoying the delicious sunshine which kissed her poor little bare feet, and seemed to wrap her all up in its warm embrace. Then she turned to her little friend.

'Cuckoo,' she said, 'I thank you *so* much. This is fairyland, at last!'

The cuckoo smiled, I was going to say, but that would be a figure of speech only, would it not? He shook his head gently.

'No, Griselda,' he said kindly; 'this is only butterfly-land.'

'*Butterfly*-land!' repeated Griselda, with a little disappointment in her tone.

'Well,' said the cuckoo, 'it's where you were wishing to be yesterday, isn't it?'

Griselda did not particularly like these allusions to 'yesterday'. She thought it would be as well to change the subject.

'It's a beautiful place, whatever it is,' she said, 'and I'm sure, cuckoo, I'm *very* much obliged to you for bringing me here. Now may I run about and look at everything? How delicious it is to feel the warm sunshine again! I didn't know how cold I was. Look, cuckoo, my toes and fingers are quite blue; they're only just beginning to come right again. I suppose the sun always shines here. How nice it must be to be a butterfly; don't you think so, cuckoo? Nothing to do but fly about.'

She stopped at last, quite out of breath.

'Griselda,' said the cuckoo, 'if you want me to answer your questions, you must ask them one at a time. You may run about and look at everything if you like, but you had better not be in such a hurry. You will make a great many mistakes if you are – you have made some already.'

'How?' said Griselda.

'*Have* the butterflies nothing to do but fly about? Watch them.'
Griselda watched.

'They do seem to be doing something,' she said, at last, 'but I can't
think what. They seem to be nibbling at the flowers, and then flying
away, something like bees gathering honey. *Butterflies* don't gather
honey, cuckoo?'

'No,' said the cuckoo. 'They are filling their paintboxes.'

'What *do* you mean?' said Griselda.

'Come and see,' said the cuckoo.

He flew quietly along in front of her, leading the way through
the prettiest paths in all the pretty garden. The paths were arranged
in different colours, as it were; that is to say, the flowers growing
along their sides were not all 'mixty-maxty', but one shade after
another in regular order – from the palest blush pink to the very
deepest damask crimson; then, again, from the soft greenish blue of
the small grass forget-me-not to the rich warm tinge of the brilliant
cornflower. *Every* tint was there; shades, to which, though not
exactly strange to her, Griselda could yet have given no name, for
the daisy dew, you see, had sharpened her eyes to observe delicate
variations of colour, as she had never done before.

'How beautifully the flowers are planned,' she said to the
cuckoo. 'Is it just to look pretty, or why?'

'It saves time,' replied the cuckoo. 'The fetch-and-carry butterflies
know exactly where to go to for the tint the world-flower-painters
want.'

'Who are the fetch-and-carry butterflies, and who are the world-
flower-painters?' asked Griselda.

'Wait a bit and you'll see, and use your eyes,' answered the cuckoo. 'It'll do your tongue no harm to have a rest now and then.'

Griselda thought it as well to take his advice, though not particularly relishing the manner in which it was given. She did use her eyes, and as she and the cuckoo made their way along the flower alleys, she saw that the butterflies were never idle. They came regularly, in little parties of twos and threes, and nibbled away, as she called it, at flowers of the same colour but different shades, till they had got what they wanted. Then off flew butterfly No. 1 with perhaps the palest tint of maize, of yellow, or lavender, whichever he was in quest of, followed by No. 2 with the next deeper shade of the

same, and No. 3 bringing up the rear.

Griselda gave a little sigh.

'What's the matter?' said the cuckoo.

'They work very hard,' she replied, in a melancholy tone.

'It's a busy time of year,' observed the cuckoo, drily.

After a while they came to what seemed to be a sort of centre to the garden. It was a huge glasshouse, with numberless doors, in and out of which butterflies were incessantly flying – reminding Griselda again of bees and a beehive. But she made no remark till the cuckoo spoke again.

'Come in,' he said.

Griselda had to stoop a good deal, but she did manage to get in without knocking her head or doing any damage. Inside was just a mass of butterflies. A confused mass it seemed at first, but after a while she saw that it was the very reverse of confused. The butterflies were all settled in rows on long, narrow, white tables, and before each was a tiny object about the size of a flattened-out pin's head, which he was most carefully painting with one of his tentacles, which, from time to time, he moistened by rubbing it on the head of a butterfly waiting patiently behind him. Behind this butterfly again stood another, who after a while took his place, while the first attendant flew away.

'To fill his paintbox again,' remarked the cuckoo, who seemed to read Griselda's thoughts.

'But what *are* they painting, cuckoo?' she inquired eagerly.

'All the flowers in the world,' replied the cuckoo. 'Autumn, winter, and spring, they're hard at work. It's only just for the three months of summer that the butterflies have any holiday, and then a few stray ones now and then wander up to the world, and people talk about "idle butterflies"! And even then it isn't true that they are idle. They go up to take a look at the flowers, to see how their work has turned out, and many a damaged petal they repair, or touch up a faded tint, though no one ever knows it.'

'*I* know it now,' said Griselda. 'I will never talk about idle butterflies again − never. But, cuckoo, do they paint all the flowers *here*, too? What a *fearful* lot they must have to do!'

'No,' said the cuckoo, 'the flowers down here are fairy flowers. They never fade or die, they are always just as you see them. But the colours of your flowers are all taken from them, as you have seen. Of course they don't look the same up there,' he went on, with a slight contemptuous shrug of his cuckoo shoulders. 'The coarse air and the ugly things about must take the bloom off. The wild flowers do

the best, to my thinking; people don't meddle with them in their stupid, clumsy way.'

'But how do they get the flowers sent up to the world, cuckoo?' asked Griselda.

'They're packed up, of course, and taken up at night when all of you are asleep,' said the cuckoo. 'They're painted on elastic stuff, you see, which fits itself as the plant grows. Why, if your eyes were as they are usually, Griselda, you couldn't even *see* the petals the butterflies are painting now.'

'And the packing up,' said Griselda, 'do the butterflies do that too?'

'No,' said the cuckoo, 'the fairies look after that.'

'How wonderful!' exclaimed Griselda. But before the cuckoo had time to say more a sudden tumult filled the air. It was butterfly dinner-time!

~

E. B. White

CHARLOTTE'S WEB

ILLUSTRATED BY GARTH WILLIAMS

THE MIRACLE

*Wilbur the pig is being fattened for market, but his dear friend Charlotte,
a beautiful grey spider, is determined to save him.*

DAY after day the spider waited, head–down, for an idea to
come to her. Hour by hour she sat motionless, deep in
thought. Having promised Wilbur that she would save his
life, she was determined to keep her promise.

Charlotte was naturally patient. She knew from experience
that if she waited long enough, a fly would come to her web;
and she felt sure that if she thought long enough about Wilbur's
problem, an idea would come to her mind.

Finally, one morning towards the middle of July, the idea
came. 'Why, how perfectly simple!' she said to herself. 'The way
to save Wilbur's life is to play a trick on Zuckerman. If I can fool
a bug,' thought Charlotte, 'I can surely fool a man. People are
not as smart as bugs.'

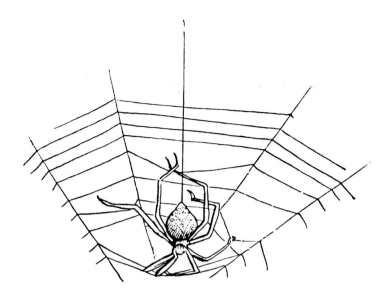

Wilbur walked into his yard just at that moment.

'What are you thinking about, Charlotte?' he asked.

'I was just thinking,' said the spider, 'that people are very gullible.'

'What does "gullible" mean?'

'Easy to fool,' said Charlotte.

'That's a mercy,' replied Wilbur, and he lay down in the shade of his fence and went fast asleep. The spider, however, stayed wide awake, gazing affectionately at him and making plans for his future. Summer was half gone. She knew she didn't have much time.

Shadows lengthened. The cool and kindly breath of evening entered through doors and windows. Astride her web, Charlotte sat moodily eating a horse-fly and thinking about the future. After a while she bestirred herself.

She descended to the centre of the web and there she began

to cut some of her lines. She worked slowly but steadily while the other creatures drowsed. None of the others, not even the goose, noticed that she was at work. Deep in his soft bed, Wilbur snoozed. Over in their favourite corner, the goslings whistled a night song.

Charlotte tore quite a section out of her web, leaving an open space in the middle. Then she started weaving something to take the place of the threads she had removed.

The next day was foggy. Everything on the farm was dripping wet. The grass looked like a magic carpet. The asparagus patch looked like a silver forest.

On foggy mornings, Charlotte's web was truly a thing of beauty. This morning each thin strand was decorated with dozens of tiny beads of water. The web glistened in the light and made a pattern of loveliness and mystery, like a delicate veil. Even Lurvy, who wasn't particularly interested in beauty, noticed the web when he came with the pig's breakfast. He noted how clearly it showed up and he noted how big and carefully built it was. And then he took another look and he saw something that made him set his pail down. There, in the centre of the web, neatly woven in block letters, was a message. It said:

SOME PIG!

Lurvy felt weak. He brushed his hand across his eyes and stared harder at Charlotte's web.

'I'm seeing things,' he whispered. He dropped to his knees and uttered a short prayer. Then, forgetting all about Wilbur's breakfast, he walked back to the house and called Mr Zuckerman.

'I think you'd better come down to the pigpen,' he said.

'What's the trouble?' asked Mr Zuckerman. 'Anything wrong with the pig?'

'No – not exactly,' said Lurvy. 'Come and see for yourself.'

The two men walked silently down to Wilbur's yard. Lurvy pointed to the spider's web. 'Do you see what I see?' he asked.

Zuckerman stared at the writing on the web. Then he murmured the words 'Some pig'. Then he looked at Lurvy. Then they both began to tremble. Charlotte, sleepy after her night's exertions, smiled as she watched.

Wilbur came and stood directly under the web.

'Some pig!' muttered Lurvy in a low voice.

'Some pig!' whispered Mr Zuckerman. They stared and stared for a long time at Wilbur. Then they stared at Charlotte.

'You don't suppose that that spider . . .' began Mr Zuckerman – but he shook his head and didn't finish the sentence. Instead, he walked solemnly back up to the house and spoke to his wife. 'Edith, something has happened,' he said, in a weak voice. He went into the living room and sat down, and Mrs Zuckerman followed.

'I've got something to tell you, Edith,' he said. 'You better sit down.'

Mrs Zuckerman sank into a chair. She looked pale and frightened.

'Edith,' he said, trying to keep his voice steady, 'I think you had best be told that we have a very unusual pig.'

A look of complete bewilderment came over Mrs Zuckerman's face. 'Homer Zuckerman, what in the world are you talking about?' she said.

'This is a very serious thing, Edith,' he replied. 'Our pig is completely out of the ordinary.'

'What's unusual about the pig?' asked Mrs Zuckerman, who was beginning to recover from her scare.

'Well, I don't really know yet,' said Mr Zuckerman. 'But we have received a sign, Edith – a mysterious sign. A miracle has happened on this farm. There is a large spider's web in the doorway of the barn cellar, right over the pigpen, and when Lurvy went to feed the pig this morning, he noticed the web because it was foggy, and you know how a spider's web looks very distinct in a fog. And right spang in the middle of the web there were the words "Some pig". The words were woven right into the web. They were actually part of the web, Edith. I know, because I have been down there and seen them. It says, "Some pig", just as clear as clear can be. There can be no mistake about it. A miracle has happened and a sign has occurred here on earth, right on our farm, and we have no ordinary pig.'

'Well,' said Mrs Zuckerman, 'it seems to me you're a little off. It seems to me we have no ordinary *spider.*'

'Oh, no,' said Zuckerman. 'It's the pig that's unusual. It says so, right there in the middle of the web.'

'Maybe so,' said Mrs Zuckerman. 'Just the same, I intend to have a look at that spider.'

'It's just a common grey spider,' said Zuckerman.

They got up, and together they walked down to Wilbur's yard. 'You see, Edith? It's just a common grey spider.'

Wilbur was pleased to receive so much attention. Lurvy was still standing there, and Mr and Mrs Zuckerman, all three, stood for about an hour, reading the words on the web over and over, and watching Wilbur.

Charlotte was delighted with the way her trick was working. She sat without moving a muscle, and listened to the conversation of the people. When a small fly blundered into the web, just beyond the word 'pig', Charlotte dropped quickly down, rolled the fly up, and carried it out of the way.

After a while the fog lifted. The web dried off and the words didn't show up so plainly. The Zuckermans and Lurvy walked back to the house. Just before they left the pigpen, Mr Zuckerman took one last look at Wilbur.

'You know,' he said, in an important voice, 'I've thought all along that that pig of ours was an extra good one. He's a solid pig. That pig is as solid as they come. You notice how solid he is around the shoulders, Lurvy?'

'Sure, sure I do,' said Lurvy. 'I've always noticed that pig. He's quite a pig.'

'He's long, and he's smooth,' said Zuckerman.

'That's right,' agreed Lurvy. 'He's as smooth as they come. He's some pig.'

Helen Cresswell

ADDING UP TO ZERO

ILLUSTRATED BY CHRIS FISHER

How Zero became part of the utterly eccentric Bagthorpe family.

YOU might like to know how that hapless mongrel, Zero, came to be part of the Bagthorpe ménage. The Bagthorpes themselves could certainly all remember the day he appeared out of nowhere in the garden, even down to the exact date.

Mr Bagthorpe said that it was the kind of date that burns itself into your brain, like the day war broke out, or the sinking of the *Titanic*, but the real reason why everybody remembered it was because it happened to have been Jack's birthday. It was this coincidence, coupled with the fact that it was Jack who actually came upon him, that seemed to make Zero, right from the very beginning, Jack's dog.

It was a fine day, and after breakfast Jack went out intending to put in some target practice with the archery set he had just received. (At the time, remember, he was only ten – all this took place over two years before the start of the first book in the Saga.)

'Just you be careful with that thing,' Mr Bagthorpe warned him. 'That is a lethal weapon. More Englishmen in the course of history have been killed by a bow and arrow than by any other weapon known to man.' (Mr Bagthorpe was always coming out with these kind of hazy statistics when he wanted to back up his own points. Jack did not see how his father could possibly have access to these figures, short of being the Archangel Gabriel. Wisely, he did not say so.)

'At present,' Mr Bagthorpe continued, 'you possess two eyes. You may not be a genius, but at least you can see where you are going. And so, at the moment, can we all. I should like to think that this family will be in possession of its full quota of eyes at the end of the day.'

The others had already announced their intention of giving Jack and his archery a wide berth, at least until he had got in some practice, and so he was alone when he first saw the dog.

It was large, very shaggy, and hiding in the hollyhocks. The two of them exchanged a long stare. Jack could not see much eye, because of a long fall of matted fur. But the longer he gazed the more he was certain that the eyes were gentle, if not actually apologetic.

'Come on,' said Jack encouragingly. 'Good boy!'

Nothing happened.

'Walkies!' he then cried hopefully.

Nothing. Just the mournful stare and general air of slump.

'He must be exhausted,' Jack thought. 'He's probably a faithful dog following his master to the ends of the earth.' Instantly he hoped not. 'Probably a faithful dog abandoned by a heartless master,' he amended. This was a better theory, because it then followed that the dog would be looking for a new master, and this could be Jack himself – which would be his wildest dream come true.

It was by now clear that the mountain would have to come to Mohammed. Jack approached the hollyhocks.

'Good boy!' he said encouragingly again. He knelt, stretched forward and patted the rough head and felt a ridiculous lump in his throat. 'Oh, you good old chap!'

Jack spent a full hour with his find before introducing him to the rest of the family. By then he was wagging his tail, though it seemed to Jack that his ears had a depressed droop, and he seemed to drag his paws rather. Jack put this down to his probably having travelled a hundred miles in search of his faithless master, and decided that a

155

square meal would soon put things right.

Unfortunately Mrs Fosdyke, who came in to help his mother in the house, was hedgehogging about in the kitchen as she always did when there was a birthday party in the offing.

'It's all right, old chap,' Jack whispered before pushing open the door. 'Her bark's worse than her bite.'

Mrs Fosdyke whirled about in her tracks. Her eyes went straight to the dog and stretched in disbelief.

'Whatever's that!' she exclaimed.

'It's a dog, Mrs Fosdyke.'

'Dog?' she echoed. 'Whatever kind of dog, I ask you, a sight like that? You mean to say they've gone and given you a *dog*?'

'He's hungry,' Jack said, dodging the question.

'I should've thought Mrs Bagthorpe'd have had more sense!' She was plainly disgusted. 'The food it'll eat, great hairy thing! And look at the size of them paws! Paws like dinner plates, it's got!'

By now Jack had found some cold meat in the fridge and was shredding it into a bowl.

'If there had to be a dog,' Mrs Fosdyke was saying, to herself mostly, 'why couldn't it've been something nice and tame, like one of them miniature poodles? Why go getting something the size of a sheep? Here – that meat's meant for sandwiches!'

'It's *my* birthday party,' Jack said boldly, 'so I think I ought to be able to give part of it away, if I like.'

It was very unlike Jack to stand up to anybody and he surprised even himself. In any case, Mrs Fosdyke had left matters too late for debate.

The bowl reached the floor, became invisible under that great tufted head, and the next minute the dog sat back on his haunches, licking his chops, and the bowl was empty.

'Well I never! What did I tell you? Near a pound of best beef! Where's its tins? Dogs is supposed to eat things out of tins.'

'Excuse me,' Jack said, 'I'm going to find Mother. Come on, boy.'

Jack felt it was important to introduce the dog to Mrs Bagthorpe before any of the rest of the family saw him. Rosie, being only six at the time, would probably think he was lovely, but the rest of them, Jack well knew, would instantly pitch into him in their usual style. Mrs Bagthorpe was really the only member of the family who could be described as soft-hearted.

He found her in the dining room laying out the table and even she was dubious when she saw the newcomer.

'He is rather large, dear,' she said. 'And in any case, I expect he already has an owner. Have you looked on his collar?'

'Yes, I have,' Jack told her. 'There's nothing. Nobody wants him. He's an outcast. *Can* I have him? Think – it's like a sign, him coming on my birthday, and I've always wanted a dog, you know I have.'

'Yes, dear, I do know. But you know what your father has always said.'

'I think even Father will like him,' said Jack stubbornly.

In this he was wrong. Mr Bagthorpe's reaction, when he emerged from his study in search of coffee and tripped over what he at first thought to be an ill-placed rug, was anything but favourable. When he had regained his balance, he turned and cast on the dog a look of utter disbelief.

'What,' he eventually demanded, 'in the name of all that is wonderful, is *that*?'

'It's a dog, Father. He's going to be mine.'

'He – is – *what*?' It was always a very bad sign when Mr Bagthorpe spaced his words out.

'He's been abandoned,' Jack said. 'An orphan, cast out into the world. He was in the garden, waiting for me. It's a sign. It is my birthday, remember.'

'It is not *my* birthday,' replied Mr Bagthorpe, unmoved, 'nor that of anyone else in this household. If that tangled bunch of paws were to remain here, it would make the life of everyone under this roof one of unremitting hell. We should all be out of our minds within the week.'

Mr Bagthorpe was by now, predictably, beginning to shout, and other members of the family soon appeared in the hope of a good row. They were not disappointed.

Grandma, who on principle always took the opposite view to

that of her son on any issue, immediately ranged herself on Jack's side.

'Jack should be allowed to keep the animal,' she declared. 'It is, I admit, of undistinguished appearance, but every normal boy should have a dog.'

'*I* never had one!' yelled Mr Bagthorpe. 'You never let me!'

'You were never a normal boy,' she replied calmly.

'Where's *mine*, then?' demanded Jack's elder brother, William. 'Why haven't *I* got a dog, then?'

'And me!' cried Tess. 'What boys can have girls can have, can't they, Mother? You're always saying so.'

'And me and me and me!' squealed Rosie. '*I* want one. I want a little one, a *little* dear puppy!'

'Now listen here!' yelled Mr Bagthorpe above the clamour. 'If this house is to be turned into a full-scale kennels, I'm off – d'you hear? If I am to be surrounded by packs of baying hounds biting everyone's legs and burying bones under the carpets and eating us out of house and home, I'm off!'

The row went on for most of the day, though when the time for the party approached Mrs Bagthorpe did manage to arrange some kind of truce. For the time being, she said, the dog could stay.

'That is only common humanity,' she said. 'But we must advertise him in the *Lost and Found* columns of the newspaper.'

'What as?' Tess wanted to know. 'What make is he?'

'Make?' Mr Bagthorpe let out one of his bitter laughs. '*Make?* You are not suggesting that *that* heap of matted fur is any breed known to the Kennel Club? It is hard even to see that it is a dog.'

He turned a withering look on the unfortunate visitor, who by now had hunched up right next to Jack, his nose buried under his enormous paws, trying to make himself invisible.

'Mutton-headed, pudding-footed hound!' he said at last. 'Even if someone *does* see the advert, they won't come forward. They'll just laugh, and sit tight. If ever I got the chance to lose a thing like that, *I'd* never come forward.'

And no one ever did. Mr Bagthorpe at least had the satisfaction of being right about that. And it was he who named the new arrival. Later that day they were discussing the question of names when it turned out that he did not even know how to fetch a stick when it was thrown.

'*All* dogs can fetch sticks,' he declared disgustedly. 'They are practically *born* being able to fetch sticks.'

'*And* he piddled on the sitting-room carpet,' chimed in Rosie.

Mr Bagthorpe groaned.

'If there was anything less than nothing, that matted-up heap of fur would be it,' he said. 'But there isn't. So Zero it is.'

And Zero it was, though in years to come he was to prove

Mr Bagthorpe wrong about him on more than one occasion, and eventually became a household word, the most famous dog in England. And that added up to something rather more than Zero.

∽

E. Nesbit

THE RAILWAY CHILDREN

ILLUSTRATED BY ROBIN BELL CORFIELD

THE END

When Father goes away unexpectedly, Roberta, Peter, Phyllis and their
mother have to leave their old home to live in a small cottage near a
country railway station. They soon make new friends at the Railway, but
no one can tell them where Father is, or when he will return.
Then one day . . .

'I WISH something would happen,' said Bobbie, dreamily, 'something wonderful.'

And something wonderful did happen exactly four days after she had said this. I wish I could say it was three days after, because in fairy tales it is always three days after that things happen. But this is not a fairy story, and besides, it really was four and not three, and I am nothing if not strictly truthful.

They seemed to be hardly Railway children at all in those days,

and as the days went on each had an uneasy feeling about this which Phyllis expressed one day.

'I wonder if the Railway misses us,' she said, plaintively. 'We never go to see it now.'

'It seems ungrateful,' said Bobbie; 'we loved it so when we hadn't anyone to play with.'

'Perks is always coming up to ask after Jim,' said Peter, 'and the signalman's little boy is better. He told me so.'

'I didn't mean the people,' explained Phyllis; 'I meant the dear Railway itself.'

'The thing I don't like,' said Bobbie, on this fourth day, which was a Tuesday, 'is having stopped waving to the 9.15 and sending our love to Father by it.'

'Let's begin again,' said Phyllis. And they did.

Somehow the change of everything that was made by having servants in the house and Mother not doing any writing made the time seem extremely long since that strange morning at the beginning of things, when they had got up so early and burnt the bottom out of the kettle and had apple pie for breakfast and first seen the Railway.

It was September now, and the turf on the slope to the Railway was dry and crisp. Little long grass spikes stood up like bits of gold wire, frail blue harebells trembled on their tough, slender stalks. Gipsy roses opened wide and flat their lilac-coloured discs, and the golden stars of St John's Wort shone at the edges of the pool that lay half-way to the Railway. Bobbie gathered a generous handful of the flowers and thought how pretty they would look lying on the green-and-pink blanket of silk waste that now covered Jim's poor broken leg.

'Hurry up,' said Peter, 'or we shall miss the 9.15!'

'I can't hurry more than I am doing,' said Phyllis. 'Oh, bother it! My bootlace has come undone *again*!'

'When you're married,' said Peter, 'your bootlace will come undone going up the church aisle, and your man that you're going to get married to will tumble over it and smash his nose in on the ornamented pavement; and then you'll say you won't marry him, and you'll have to be an old maid.'

'I shan't,' said Phyllis. 'I'd much rather marry a man with his nose smashed in than not marry anybody.'

'It would be horrid to marry a man with a smashed nose all the same,' went on Bobbie. 'He wouldn't be able to smell the flowers at the wedding. Wouldn't that be awful!'

'Bother the flowers at the wedding!' cried Peter. 'Look! The signal's down. We must run!'

They ran. And once more they waved their handkerchiefs without at all minding whether the handkerchiefs were clean or not, to the 9.15.

'Take our love to Father!' cried Bobbie. And the others, too,

shouted: 'Take our love to Father!'

The old gentleman waved from his first-class carriage window. Quite violently he waved. And there was nothing odd in that, for he always had waved. But what was really remarkable was that from every window handkerchiefs fluttered, newspapers signalled, hands waved wildly. The train swept by with a rustle and roar, the little pebbles jumped and danced under it as it passed, and the children were left looking at each other.

'Well!' said Peter.

'*Well!*' said Bobbie.

'WELL!' said Phyllis.

'Whatever on earth does that mean?' asked Peter, but he did not expect any answer.

'I *don't* know,' said Bobbie. 'Perhaps the old gentleman told the people at his station to look out for us and wave. He knew we should like it!'

Now, curiously enough, this was just what had happened. The old gentleman, who was very well known and respected at this particular station, had got there early this morning, and he had waited at the door where the young man stands holding the interesting machine that clips the tickets, and he had said something to every single passenger who passed through that door. And after nodding to what the old gentleman had said – after the nods expressed every shade of surprise, interest, doubt, cheerful pleasure, and grumpy agreement – each passenger had gone on to the platform and read one certain part of his newspaper. And when the passengers got into the train, they had told the other passengers who were already there what the old gentleman had said, and then the other passengers had also looked at their newspapers and seemed very astonished and, mostly, pleased. Then, when the train passed the fence where the three children were, newspapers and hands and handkerchiefs were waved madly, till all that side of the train was fluttery with white, like pictures of the King's Coronation in the biography at Maskelyne and Cook's. To the children it almost seemed as though the train itself was alive, and was at last responding to the love that they had given it so freely and so long.

'It is most extraordinarily rum!' said Peter.

'Most stronery!' echoed Phyllis.

But Bobbie said, 'Don't you think the old gentleman's waves seemed more significating than usual?'

'No,' said the others.

'I do,' said Bobbie. 'I thought he was trying to explain something to us with his newspaper.'

'Explain what?' asked Peter, not unnaturally.

'*I* don't know,' Bobbie answered, 'but I do feel most awfully funny. I feel just exactly as if something was going to happen.'

'What is going to happen,' said Peter, 'is that Phyllis's stocking is going to come down.'

This was but too true. The suspender had given way in the agitation of the waves to the 9.15. Bobbie's handkerchief served as first aid to the injured, and they all went home.

Lessons were more than usually

difficult to Bobbie that day. Indeed, she disgraced herself so deeply over a quite simple sum about the division of 48 pounds of meat and 36 pounds of bread among 144 hungry children that Mother looked at her anxiously.

'Don't you feel quite well, dear?' she asked.

'I don't know,' was Bobbie's unexpected answer. 'I don't know how I feel. It isn't that I'm lazy. Mother, will you let me off lessons today? I feel as if I wanted to be quite alone by myself.'

'Yes, of course I'll let you off,' said Mother: 'but —'

Bobbie dropped her slate. It cracked just across the little green mark that is so useful for drawing patterns round, and it was never the same slate again. Without waiting to pick it up she bolted. Mother caught her in the hall feeling blindly among the waterproofs and umbrellas for her garden hat.

'What is it, my sweetheart?' said Mother. 'You don't feel ill, do you?'

'I *don't* know,' Bobbie answered, a little breathlessly, 'but I want to be by myself and see if my head really *is* all silly and my inside all squirmy-twisty.'

'Hadn't you better lie down?' Mother said, stroking her hair back from her forehead.

'I'd be more alive in the garden, I think,' said Bobbie.

But she could not stay in the garden. The hollyhocks and the asters and the late roses all seemed to be waiting for something to happen. It was one of those still, shiny autumn days, when everything does seem to be waiting.

Bobbie could not wait.

'I'll go down to the station,' she said, 'and talk to Perks and ask about the signalman's little boy.'

So she went down. On the way she passed the old lady from the Post-office, who gave her a kiss and a hug, but rather to Bobbie's surprise, no words except: 'God bless you, love –' and, after a pause, 'Run along – do.'

The draper's boy, who had sometimes been a little less than civil and a little more than contemptuous, now touched his cap, and uttered the remarkable words: "Morning, Miss. I'm sure –'

The blacksmith, coming along with an open newspaper in his hand, was even more strange in his manner. He grinned broadly, though, as a rule, he was a man not given to smiles, and waved the newspaper long before he came up to her. And as he passed her, he said, in answer to her 'Good morning': 'Good morning to you, Missie, and many of them! I wish you joy, that I do!'

'Oh!' said Bobbie to herself, and her heart quickened its beats, 'something *is* going to happen! I know it is – everyone is so odd, like people are in dreams.'

The Station Master wrung her hand warmly. In fact he worked it up and down like a pump-handle. But he gave her no reason for this unusually enthusiastic greeting. He only said: 'The 11.54's a bit late, Miss – the extra luggage this holiday time,' and went away very quickly into that inner Temple of his into which even Bobbie dared not follow him.

Perks was not to be seen, and Bobbie shared the solitude of the platform with the Station Cat. This tortoise-shell lady, usually of a retiring disposition, came today to rub herself against the brown stockings of Bobbie with arched back, waving tail, and reverberating purrs.

'Dear me!' said Bobbie, stooping to stroke her, 'how very kind everybody is today – even you, pussy!'

Perks did not appear until the 11.54 was signalled, and then he, like everybody else that morning, had a newspaper in his hand.

'Hullo!' he said, ''ere you are. Well, if *this* is the train, it'll be smart work! Well, God bless you, my dear! I see it in the paper, and I don't think I was ever so glad of anything in all my born days!' He looked at Bobbie a moment, then said, 'One I must have, Miss, and no offence, I know, on a day like this 'ere!' and with that he kissed her, first on one cheek and then on the other.

'You ain't offended, are you?' he asked anxiously. 'I ain't took too great a liberty? On a day like this, you know –'

'No, no,' said Bobbie, 'of course it's not a liberty, dear Mr Perks; we love you quite as much as if you were an uncle of ours – but – on a day like *what*?'

'Like this 'ere!' said Perks. 'Don't I tell you I see it in the paper?'

'Saw *what* in the paper?' asked Bobbie, but already the 11.54 was steaming into the station and the Station Master was looking at all the places where Perks was not and ought to have been.

Bobbie was left standing alone, the Station Cat watching her from under the bench with friendly golden eyes.

Of course you know already exactly what was going to happen. Bobbie was not so clever. She had the vague, confused, expectant feeling that comes to one's heart in dreams. What her heart expected I can't tell – perhaps the very thing that you and I know was going to happen – but her mind expected nothing; it was almost blank, and felt nothing but tiredness and stupidness and an empty feeling like your body has when you have been a long walk and it is very far indeed past your proper dinnertime.

Only three people got out of the 11.54. The first was a countrywoman with two baskety boxes full of live chickens who stuck their russet heads out anxiously through the wicker bars; the second was Miss Peckitt, the grocer's wife's cousin, with a tin box and three brown-paper parcels; and the third –

'Oh! My Daddy, my Daddy!' That scream went like a knife into the heart of everyone in the train, and people put their heads out of the windows to see a tall pale man with lips set in a thin close line, and a little girl clinging to him with arms and legs, while his arms went tightly round her.

Anna Sewell

BLACK BEAUTY

ILLUSTRATED BY RICHARD JONES

POOR GINGER

Black Beauty tells the story of his life over a hundred years ago in Victorian England. Some of Beauty's memories are happy, some are sad, but few are as moving as when he meets his old friend Ginger.

ONE day, whilst our cab and many others were waiting outside one of the Parks, where a band was playing, a shabby old cab drove up beside ours. The horse was an old worn-out chestnut, with an ill-kept coat, and bones that showed plainly through it. The knees knuckled over, and the forelegs were very unsteady. I had been eating some hay, and the wind rolled a little lock of it that way, and the poor creature put out her long thin neck and picked it up, and then turned round and looked about for more. There was a hopeless look in the dull eye that I could not help noticing, and then, as I was thinking where I had seen that horse before, she looked full at me and said, 'Black Beauty, is that you?'

It was Ginger! But how changed! The beautifully arched and

glossy neck was now straight and lank, and fallen in, the clean straight legs and delicate fetlocks were swelled; the joints were grown out of shape with hard work; the face, that was once so full of spirit and life, was now full of suffering, and I could tell by the heaving of her sides, and her frequent cough, how bad her breath was.

Our drivers were standing together a little way off, so I sidled up to her a step or two, that we might have a little quiet talk. It was a sad tale that she had to tell.

After a twelvemonth's run off at Earlshall, she was considered to be fit for work again, and was sold to a gentleman. For a little while she got on very well, but after a longer gallop than usual the old strain returned, and after being rested and doctored she was again sold. In this way she changed hands several times, but always getting lower down.

'And so at last,' said she, 'I was bought by a man who keeps a number of cabs and horses, and lets them out. You look well off, and I am glad of it, but I could not tell you what my life has been. When they found out my weakness, they said I was not worth what they gave for me, and that I must go into one of the low cabs, and just be used up; that is what they are doing, whipping and working me with never one thought of what I suffer; they paid for me, and must get it out of me, they say. The man who hires me now pays a deal of money to the owner every day, and so he has to get it out of me too; and so it's all the week round and round, with never a Sunday rest.'

I said, 'You used to stand up for yourself if you were ill-used.'

'Ah!' she said, 'I did once, but it's no use; men are strongest, and if they are cruel and have no feeling, there is nothing that we can do, but just bear it, bear it on and on to the end. I wish the end was come, I wish I was dead. I have seen dead horses, and I am sure they do not suffer pain. I wish I may drop down dead at my work, and not be sent off to the knacker's.'

I was very much troubled, and I put my nose up to hers, but I could say nothing to comfort her. I think she was pleased to see me, for she said, 'You are the only friend I ever had.'

Just then her driver came up, and with a tug at her mouth backed her out of the line and drove off, leaving me very sad indeed.

A short time after this a cart with a dead horse in it passed our cab-stand. The head hung out of the cart-tail, the lifeless tongue was slowly dropping with blood; and the sight was too dreadful. It was a chestnut horse with a long thin neck. I saw a white streak down the forehead. I believe it was Ginger; I hoped it was, for then her troubles would be over. Oh! If men were more merciful, they would shoot us before we came to such misery.

J. R. R. Tolkien

THE HOBBIT

ILLUSTRATED BY CHRIS RIDDELL

INSIDE INFORMATION

Bilbo Baggins, a hobbit, joins a band of dwarves looking for their ancient treasure. After many adventures they arrive at the lair of Smaug, a terrible dragon. Bilbo is chosen to explore the cave.

AFTER a while Balin bade Bilbo 'Good luck!' and stopped where he could still see the faint outline of the door, and by a trick of the echoes of the tunnel hear the rustle of the whispering voices of the others just outside. Then the hobbit slipped on his ring, and warned by the echoes to take more than hobbit's care to make no sound, he crept noiselessly down, down, down into the dark. He was trembling with fear, but his little face was set and grim. Already he was a very different hobbit from the one that had run out without a pocket-handkerchief from Bag-End long ago. He had not had a pocket-handkerchief for ages. He loosened his dagger in its sheath, tightened his belt, and went on.

★

'Now you are in for it at last, Bilbo Baggins,' he said to himself. 'You went and put your foot right in it that night of the party, and now you have got to pull it out and pay for it! Dear me, what a fool I was and am!' said the least Tookish part of him. 'I have absolutely no use for dragon-guarded treasures, and the whole lot could stay here for ever, if only I could wake up and find this beastly tunnel was my own front-hall at home!'

He did not wake up of course, but went still on and on, till all sign of the door behind had faded away. He was altogether alone. Soon he thought it was beginning to feel warm. 'Is that a kind of a glow I seem to see coming right ahead down there?' he thought.

It was. As he went forward it grew and grew, till there was no doubt about it. It was a red light steadily getting redder and redder. Also it was now undoubtedly hot in the tunnel. Wisps of vapour floated up and past him and he began to sweat. A sound, too, began to throb in his ears, a sort of bubbling like the noise of a large pot galloping on the fire, mixed with a rumble as of a gigantic tom-cat purring. This grew to the unmistakable gurgling noise of some vast animal snoring in its sleep down there in the red glow in front of him.

It was at this point that Bilbo stopped. Going on from there was the bravest thing he ever did. The tremendous things that happened afterwards were as nothing compared to it. He fought the real battle in that tunnel alone, before he ever saw the vast danger that lay in wait. At any rate after a short halt go on he did; and you can picture him coming to the end of the tunnel, an opening of much the same size and shape as the door above. Through it peeps the hobbit's little head. Before him lies that great bottom-most cellar or

dungeon-hole of the ancient dwarves right at the mountain's root. It is almost dark so that its vastness can only be dimly guessed, but rising from the near side of the rocky floor there is a great glow. The glow of Smaug!

There he lay, a vast red-golden dragon, fast asleep; a thrumming came from his jaws and nostrils, and wisps of smoke, but his fires were low in slumber. Beneath him, under all his limbs and his huge coiled tail, and about him on all sides stretching away across the unseen floors, lay countless piles of precious things, gold wrought and unwrought, gems and jewels, and silver red-stained in the ruddy light.

Smaug lay, with wings folded like an immeasurable bat, turned partly on one side, so that the hobbit could see his underparts and his long pale belly crusted with gems and fragments of gold from his long lying on his costly bed. Behind him where the walls were nearest could dimly be seen coats of mail, helms and axes, swords and spears hanging; and there in rows stood great jars and vessels filled with a wealth that could not be guessed.

To say that Bilbo's breath was taken away is no description at all. There are no words left to express his staggerment, since Men changed the language that they learned of elves in the days when all the world was wonderful. Bilbo had heard tell and sing of dragon-hoards before, but the splendour, the lust, the glory of such treasure had never yet come home to him. His heart was filled and pierced with enchantment and with the desire of dwarves; and he gazed motionless, almost forgetting the frightful guardian, at the gold beyond price and count.

★

He gazed for what seemed an age, before, drawn almost against his will, he stole from the shadow of the doorway, across the floor to the nearest edge of the mounds of treasure. Above him the sleeping dragon lay, a dire menace even in his sleep. He grasped a great two-handled cup, as heavy as he could carry, and cast one fearful eye upwards. Smaug stirred a wing, opened a claw, the rumble of his snoring changed its note.

Then Bilbo fled. But the dragon did not wake – not yet – but shifted into other dreams of greed and violence, lying there in his stolen hall while the little hobbit toiled back up the long tunnel. His heart was beating and a more fevered shaking was in his legs than when he was going down, but still he clutched the cup, and his chief

thought was: 'I've done it! This will show them. "More like a grocer than a burglar" indeed! Well, we'll hear no more of that.'

Nor did he. Balin was overjoyed to see the hobbit again, and as delighted as he was surprised. He picked Bilbo up and carried him out into the open air. It was midnight and clouds had covered the stars, but Bilbo lay with his eyes shut, gasping and taking pleasure in the feel of fresh air again, and hardly noticing the excitement of the dwarves, or how they praised him and patted him on the back and put themselves and all their families for generations to come at his service.

The dwarves were still passing the cup from hand to hand and talking delightedly of the recovery of their treasure, when suddenly a vast rumbling woke in the mountain underneath as if it was an old volcano that had made up its mind to start eruptions once again. The door behind them was pulled nearly to, and blocked from closing with a stone, but up the long tunnel came the dreadful echoes, from far down in the depths, of a bellowing and a trampling that made the ground beneath them tremble.

Then the dwarves forgot their joy and their confident boasts of a moment before and cowered down in fright. Smaug was still to be reckoned with. It does not do to leave a live dragon out of your calculations, if you live near him. Dragons may not have much real use for all their wealth, but they know it to an ounce as a rule, especially after long possession; and Smaug was no exception. He had passed from an uneasy dream (in which a warrior, altogether insignificant in size but provided with a bitter sword and great courage, figured most unpleasantly) to a doze, and from a doze to wide waking. There was a breath of strange air in his cave. Could there be a draught from that little hole? He had never felt quite happy about it, though it was so small, and now he glared at it in suspicion and wondered why he had never blocked it up. Of late he had half fancied he had caught the dim echoes of a knocking sound from far above that came down through it to his lair. He stirred and stretched forth his neck to sniff. Then he missed the cup!

Thieves! Fire! Murder! Such a thing had not happened since first he came to the mountain! His rage passes description – the sort of rage that is only seen when rich folk that have more than they can enjoy suddenly lose something that they have long had but have never before used or wanted. His fire belched forth, the hall smoked, he shook the mountain-roots. He thrust his head in vain at the little hole, and then coiling his length together, roaring like thunder underground, he sped from his deep lair through its great door, out into the huge passages of the mountain-palace and up towards the Front Gate.

To hunt the whole mountain till he had caught the thief and had torn and trampled him was his one thought. He issued from the gate, the waters rose in fierce whistling steam, and up he soared blazing into the air and settled on the mountain-top in a spout of green and scarlet flame.

Catherine Storr

CLEVER POLLY AND THE STUPID WOLF

ILLUSTRATED BY CHRIS FISHER

LITTLE POLLY RIDING HOOD

Clever Polly isn't frightened of the hungry but inexperienced wolf.
She outwits him at every turn.

ONCE every two weeks Polly went over to the other side of the town to see her grandmother. Sometimes she took a small present, and sometimes she came back with a small present for herself. Sometimes all the rest of the family went too, and sometimes Polly went alone.

One day, when she was going by herself, she had hardly got down the front door steps when she saw the wolf.

'Good afternoon, Polly,' said the wolf. 'Where are you going to, may I ask?'

'Certainly,' said Polly. 'I'm going to see my grandma.'

'I thought so!' said the wolf, looking very much pleased. 'I've been reading about a little girl who went to visit her grandmother and it's a very good story.'

'Little Red Riding Hood?' suggested Polly.

'That's it!' cried the wolf. 'I read it out loud to myself as a bedtime story. I did enjoy it. The wolf eats up the grandmother, *and* Little Red Riding Hood. It's almost the only story where a wolf really gets anything to eat,' he added sadly.

'But in my book he doesn't get Red Riding Hood,' said Polly. 'Her father comes in just in time to save her.'

'Oh, he doesn't in *my* book!' said the wolf. 'I expect mine is the true story, and yours is just invented. Anyway, it seems a good idea.'

'What is a good idea?' asked Polly.

'To catch little girls on their way to their grandmothers' cottages,' said the wolf. 'Now where had I got to?'

'I don't know what you mean,' said Polly.

'Well, I'd said, "Where are you going to?",' said the wolf. 'Oh yes. Now I must say, "Where does she live?" Where does your grandmother live, Polly Riding Hood?'

'Over the other side of the town,' answered Polly.

The wolf frowned.

'It ought to be "Through the Wood",' he said. 'But perhaps town will do. How do you get there, Polly Riding Hood?'

'First I take a train and then I take a bus,' said Polly.

The wolf stamped his foot.

'No, no, no, no!' he shouted. 'That's all wrong. You can't say that. You've got to say, "By that path winding through the trees", or something like that. You can't go by trains and buses and things. It isn't fair.'

'Well, I could say that,' said Polly, 'but it wouldn't be true. I do have to go by bus and train to see my grandma, so what's the good of saying I don't?'

'But then it won't work,' said the wolf impatiently. 'How can I get there first and gobble her up and get all dressed up to trick you into believing I am her, if we've got a great train journey to do? And

anyhow I haven't any money on me, so I can't even take a ticket. You just can't say that.'

'All right, I won't say it,' said Polly agreeably. 'But it's true all the same. Now just excuse me, Wolf, I've got to get down to the station because I am going to visit my grandma even if you aren't.'

The wolf slunk along behind Polly, growling to himself. He stood just behind her at the booking-office and heard her ask for her ticket, but he could not go any further. Polly got into a train and was carried away, and the wolf went sadly home.

But just two weeks later the wolf was waiting outside Polly's house again. This time he had plenty of change in his pocket. He even had a book tucked under his front leg to read in the train.

He partly hid himself behind a corner of brick wall and watched to see Polly come out on her way to her grandmother's house.

But Polly did not come out alone, as she had before. This time the whole family appeared, Polly's father and mother too. They got into the car which was waiting in the road, and Polly's father started the engine.

The wolf ran along behind his brick wall as fast as he could, and was just in time to get out into the road ahead of the car, and to stand waving his paws as if he wanted a lift as the car came up.

Polly's father slowed down, and Polly's mother put her head out of the window.

'Where do you want to go?' she asked.

'I want to go to Polly's grandmother's house,' the wolf answered. His eyes glistened as he looked at the family of plump little girls in the back of the car.

'That's where we are going,' said her mother, surprised. 'Do you know her then?'

'Oh no,' said the wolf. 'But you see, I want to get there very quickly and eat her up and then I can put on her clothes and wait for Polly, and eat her up too.'

'Good heavens!' said Polly's father. 'What a horrible idea! We certainly shan't give you a lift if that is what you are planning to do.'

Polly's mother screwed up the window again and Polly's father drove quickly on. The wolf was left standing miserably in the road.

'Bother!' he said to himself angrily. 'It's gone wrong again. I can't think why it can't be the same as the Little Red Riding Hood story. It's all these buses and cars and trains that make it go wrong.'

But the wolf was determined to get Polly, and when she was due

188

to visit her grandmother again, a fortnight later, he went down and took a ticket for the station he had heard Polly ask for. When he got out of the train, he climbed on a bus, and soon he was walking down the road where Polly's grandmother lived.

'Aha!' he said to himself, 'this time I shall get them both. First the grandma, then Polly.'

He unlatched the gate into the garden, and strolled up the path to Polly's grandmother's front door. He rapped sharply with the knocker.

'Who's there?' called a voice from inside the house.

The wolf was very much pleased. This was going just as it had in the story. This time there would be no mistakes.

'Little Polly Riding Hood,' he said in a squeaky voice. 'Come to see her dear grandmother, with a little present of butter and eggs and – er – cake!'

There was a long pause. Then the voice said doubtfully, '*Who* did you say it was?'

'Little Polly Riding Hood,' said the wolf in a great hurry, quite forgetting to disguise his voice this time. 'Come to eat up her dear grandmother with butter and eggs!'

There was an even longer pause. Then Polly's grandmother put her head out of a window and looked down at the wolf.

'I beg your pardon?' she said.

'I am Polly,' said the wolf firmly.

'Oh,' said Polly's grandma. She appeared to be thinking hard. 'Good afternoon, Polly. Do you know if anyone else happens to be coming to see me today? A wolf, for instance?'

'No. Yes,' said the wolf in great confusion. 'I met a Polly as I was

coming here — I mean, I, Polly, met a wolf on my way here, but she can't have got here yet because I started specially early.'

'That's very queer,' said the grandma. 'Are you quite sure you are Polly?'

'Quite sure,' said the wolf.

'Well, then, I don't know who it is who is here already,' said Polly's grandma. 'She said she was Polly. But if you are Polly then I think this other person must be a wolf.'

'No, no, I am Polly,' said the wolf. 'And, anyhow, you ought not to say all that. You ought to say, "Lift the latch and come in."'

'I don't think I'll do that,' said Polly's grandma. 'Because I don't want my nice little Polly eaten up by a wolf, and if you come in now the wolf who is here already might eat you up.'

Another head looked out of another window. It was Polly's.

'Bad luck, Wolf,' she said. 'You didn't know that I was coming to lunch and tea today instead of just tea as I generally do — so I got here first. And as you are Polly, as you've just said, I must be the wolf, and you'd better run away quickly before I gobble you up, hadn't you?'

'Bother, bother, bother and *bother*!' said the wolf. 'It hasn't worked out right this time either. And I did just what it said in the book. Why can't I ever get you, Polly, when that other wolf managed to get his little girl?'

'Because this isn't a fairy story,' said Polly, 'and I'm not Little Red Riding Hood, I am Polly and I can always escape from you, Wolf, however much you try to catch me.'

'Clever Polly,' said Polly's grandma. And the wolf went growling away.

∽

Mary Norton

BEDKNOB AND BROOMSTICK

ILLUSTRATED BY PAUL HOWARD

THE 'PAST'

One summer Carey, Charles and Paul are sent to stay with an aunt, Miss Price. Life is a little dull – until they find out that Miss Price is learning magic. To their great delight she casts a spell on the knob of Paul's bed. He has only to twist it and wish and the bed will take them anywhere, even into the past.

IN London, during the reign of King Charles II, there lived a necromancer. (★★★★★★ These six stars are to give you time to ask what is a necromancer. Now you know, we will go on.) He lived in a little house in Cripplegate in a largish room at the top of a narrow flight of stairs. He was a very nervous man, and disliked the light of day. There were two good reasons for this; I will tell you the first.

When he was a boy he had been apprenticed to another

necromancer, an old man from whom he had inherited the business. The old necromancer, in private life, was fat and jolly, but in the presence of his clients he became solemn as an owl, and clothed his fat whiteness in a long dark robe edged with fur, so that he could fill them with respect and awe. Without his smile, and in his long dark robe, he looked as important as a mayor and as gloomy as a lawyer's clerk.

The young necromancer, whose name was Emelius Jones, worked very hard to learn his trade. It was he who had to turn out at ten to twelve on cold moonlight nights to collect cats from graveyards, and walk the lonely beaches in the grey dawn seeking seven white stones of equal size, wet by the last wave of the neap tide. It was he who had to mash up herbs with pestle and mortar and crawl down drains after rats.

The old necromancer would sit by the fire, with his feet on a footstool, drinking hot sack with a dash of cinnamon, and nod his head saying: 'Well done, my boy, well done . . .'

The young necromancer would work for hours by candlelight, studying the chart of the heavens and learning to read the stars. He would twist the globe on the ebony stand until his brain too rotated on its own axis. On sweltering afternoons he would be sent out to the country on foot to trudge through the fading heather, seeking blind-worms and adders and striped snails. He had to climb belfries after bats, rob churches for tallow, and blow down glass tubes at green slime till the blood sang in his ears and his eyes bulged.

When the old necromancer was dying he sent for his assistant and said: 'My boy, there is something I should tell you.'

Emelius folded his stained hands in his lap and dropped his tired eyes respectfully. 'Yes, sir,' he murmured.

The old necromancer moved his head so that it fitted more comfortably into the pillow.

'It's about magic,' he said.

'Yes, sir,' replied Emelius soberly.

The old necromancer smiled slyly at the carved ceiling. 'There isn't such a thing.'

Emelius raised a pair of startled eyes. 'You mean —?' he began.

'I mean,' said the old necromancer calmly, 'what I say.'

When Emelius had got over the first sense of shock (he never completely recovered) the old necromancer went on: 'All the same, it's a good paying business. I've kept a wife and five daughters out at Deptford (whence I shall be carried tomorrow), with a carriage and four, fifteen servants, French music teacher and a barque on the river. Three daughters have married well. I have two sons-in-law at court, and a third in Lombard Street.' He sighed. 'Your poor father, may he rest in peace, paid me handsomely for your apprenticeship; if I have been hard on you it is from a sense of duty towards one who is no more. My affairs are in good order, my family well provided for, so the business as it stands and these premises I leave to you.' He folded his hands on his chest and became silent.

'But,' stammered Emelius, 'I know nothing. The love philtres –'

'Coloured water,' said the old necromancer in a tired voice.

'And foretelling the future?'

'Child's play: if you don't go into details, whatever you prophesy about the future comes true sooner or later, and what doesn't come true, they forget. Look solemn, don't clean out the room more than once a year, brush up your Latin, oil the globe so that it spins smoothly – and may good luck attend you.'

That is the first reason why Emelius was a nervous type of man. The second was because in the reign of good King Charles it was still the fashion to send witches, sorcerers, and all those who were reputed to work magic to the gallows, and Emelius, if he made a slip or an enemy, might at any moment be delivered by an unsatisfied client to a very tight and uncomfortable end.

He would have got out of the business if he dared, but all the money of his patrimony had been dispensed in learning magic and he was not a strong enough character to start afresh.

In the year 1666 Emelius, at thirty-five, had become old before his time, old and thin and terribly nervous. He would jump if a mouse squeaked, turn pale at a moonbeam, tremble at his servant's knock.

If he heard a footstep on the stairs he would immediately begin a little spell, something he knew by heart, so that his clients might be impressed by his practice of magic. He had also to be ready to sit down at the clavichord, in case it was a king's man come to spy upon him, and pretend he was a dreamy musician who had inherited the necromancer's lodging.

One evening, hearing footsteps in the narrow hall below the

stairs, he leapt up from the chair where he had been dozing by the fire (these late August nights held the first chill of autumn), trod on the cat (which let out an unearthly squeal), and seized a couple of dried frogs and a bunch of henbane. He lit a wick which floated in a bowl of oil, sprinkled it with yellow powder, so it burned with a blue flame, and hurriedly, with trembling hands, rushed off a little spell – with one eye on the clavichord and the other on the door, and all his body poised for instant flight.

There was a knock, a hesitatingly fumbled knock.

'Who's there?' he called, preparing to blow out the blue flame.

There was a whisper and some shuffling, then a voice, clear and treble as a silver bell, said: 'Three children who are lost.'

Emelius was taken aback. He made a movement towards the

197

clavichord, then he came back to the blue flame. Finally, he stood between the two, with one hand carelessly poised upon the globe, in the other a sheet of music. 'Enter,' he said sombrely.

The door opened and there, thrown into relief against the dark passage-way, stood three children, strangely dressed and dazzlingly fair. They wore long robes after the style of the London apprentice, but tied by silken cords, and their cleanliness, in seventeenth-century London, seemed not of this world. Their skins shone and Emelius's quivering nostrils detected a delicate fragrance, as of fresh flowers strangely spiced.

Emelius began to tremble. His knees felt unsteady. He wanted to sit down. Instead he looked unbelievingly towards the paraphernalia of his spell. Could two dried frogs and a bunch of henbane do this? He tried to recall the gabble of Latin he had said over them.

'We are lost,' said the female child in that strange foreign voice,

clear-cut as rock crystal. 'We saw your light burning, the street door was open, so we came up to ask the way.'

'Where to?' asked Emelius in a trembling voice.

'Anywhere,' said the female child. 'We are quite lost. We don't know where we are.'

Emelius cleared his throat. 'You are in Cripplegate,' he managed to say.

'Cripplegate?' said the female child wonderingly. 'In London?'

'Yes, in London,' whispered Emelius, edging away towards the fireplace. He was terribly afraid. From whence had they come, if they did not know they were in London?

The elder male child took a step forward. 'Excuse me,' he said, very civilly, 'could you possibly tell us what century we are in?'

Emelius threw up trembling hands before his face, as if to ward off the sight of them. 'Go back, go back,' he implored, in a voice broken by emotion, 'from whence you came.'

The female child turned pink and blinked her eyelids. She looked round the dim and cluttered room, with its yellowing parchments, its glass vials, the skull on the table, and the candle-lit clavichord.

'I'm sorry,' she said, 'if we are disturbing you.'

Emelius ran to the table. He picked up the bowl with oil, the two frogs, the twisted henbane, and with an oath he threw them on the fire. They spluttered, then flared up. Emelius rubbed his fingers together as he watched the blaze, as if to rid them of some impurity. Then he turned, and again his eyes widened so that the whites showed. He stared at the children.

'Still here?' he exclaimed hoarsely.

The female child blinked her eyes faster. 'We will go at once,' she

said, 'if you would just tell us first what year it is —'

'The 27th day of August, in the year of Our Lord 1666.'

'1666,' repeated the elder male child. 'King Charles the Second —'

'The Fire of London will take place in a week's time,' said the girl child brightly, as if she were pleased.

The elder male child's face lit up too.

'Cripplegate?' he said excitedly. 'This house may be burnt. It will start at the king's baker's in Pudding Lane, and go on down Fish Street —'

Emelius suddenly fell on his knees. He clasped his hands together. His face was anguished. 'I implore you,' he cried, 'go, go . . . go . . .'

The girl child looked at him. Suddenly she smiled, with kindness, as if she understood his fear. 'We won't harm you,' she said, coming towards him. 'We're only children — feel my hand.'

She laid her hand on Emelius's clasped ones. It was warm and soft and human. 'We're only children —' she repeated. 'Out of the future,' she added. She smiled at her companions as if she had said something clever.

'Yes,' said the elder boy, looking pleased and rather surprised. 'That's what we are, just children out of the future.'

'Is that all?' said Emelius weakly. He got to his feet. He spoke rather bitterly. He felt very shaken.

Now the youngest child stepped forward. He had a face like an angel with dark gold hair above a white brow. 'Could I see your stuffed alligator?' he asked politely.

Emelius unhooked the stuffed alligator from the ceiling and laid it down on the table without a word. Then he sat down in the chair by the fire. He was shivering a little as if with cold. 'What else is about to come upon us,' he asked gloomily, 'besides the fire which will burn this house?'

The little girl sat down on a footstool opposite him. 'We're not awfully good at history,' she said in her strange way. 'But I think your king gets executed.'

'That was Charles the First,' the elder boy pointed out.

'Oh yes,' said the little girl. 'I'm sorry. We could go back and look it all up.'

'Do not give yourselves this trouble,' said Emelius glumly.

There was a short silence. The little girl broke it.

'Have you had the plague?' she asked conversationally.

Emelius shuddered. 'No – thanks be to a merciful Providence.'

'Good show,' exclaimed the elder boy heartily.

The little girl asking permission, poked the fire to a brighter blaze. Emelius threw on another log. He stared miserably at the broken bowl blackened by burning oil. The old necromancer had doubly deceived him, for he, Emelius, quite by accident, had found a spell that worked. These children seemed comparatively harmless, but another mixture, lightly thrown together in the same irresponsible way, might produce anything – from a herd of hobgoblins to Old Nick himself.

And it wasn't as if he knew the antidotes. Whatever came would come to stay. He would never feel safe again. Never more would he dare throw sulphur on the fire with muttered imprecations; never more would he dare boil soups of frogs' spawn and digitalis; never more reel off Latin curses or spin the globe of the heavens into a dizzy whirl of prophecy. His uncertainty would manifest itself before his clients. His practice would fall off. His victims might turn against him. Then he would have to fly, to hide in some filthy hovel or rat-infested cellar, or it might mean prison, the pillory, the horse-pond or the rope.

Emelius groaned and dropped his head into his hands.

Kathleen Hale

ORLANDO
THE MARMALADE CAT

ILLUSTRATED BY THE AUTHOR

A CAMPING HOLIDAY

O RLANDO was very beautiful, striped like marmalade and the same colour; his eyes reminded you of twin green gooseberries. He and his dear wife Grace had three kittens – the Tortoiseshell Pansy, snow-white Blanche and coal-black Tinkle.

Orlando wanted to take his family camping, but his Master said, 'Think of the mischief the mice will do if you go away.' Orlando told him they must have a holiday, so Master said he would think about it.

He walked up and down the lawn, thinking deeply, anxiously watched by the cats. At last he went indoors and telephoned for a pale green tent, and they knew he was going to let them go.

'Now, my dears,' said Orlando, 'I have written a list of the things we must take with us, and as I read it out you must collect them and I will pack them in the car.' Grace and the kittens did as they were told. When everything was ready, the kittens put on goggles to keep the dust out of their eyes.

Grace wore a hat and veil because she hated to have her whiskers blown into sixes and sevens by the wind. Orlando took an eye-shade only, because he liked to travel light.

'Now we're off!' purred Grace with a sigh of pleasure. She was glad to get away from house-work for a real holiday.

After motoring all morning the cats felt hungry and stopped at a farm to have a drink of milk.

The Farmer's wife said they could sit against her hay-rick to eat their sandwiches. 'But no smoking, mind,' she said, 'or you will set the rick on fire.'

After the picnic was over, the cats set off once more, each kitten with a bar of milk chocolate to lick.

'Now we must find a good camping place,' Orlando said. 'It must be near a stream but not in a swamp, of course.'

They found a patch of high ground, flat as a table and dry as a bone.

It was a perfect spot for the tent, beside a stream full of little fish and clear water to drink; wild orchids and mushrooms grew in the grass, and there was a farm nearby where the cats could buy milk.

'Fish for dinner!' purred Grace.

'Eggs for tea!' mewed Pansy from a tree-top, where she had found some in a nest.

'And water to drink,' sneezed Blanche crossly, for she had fallen into the stream.

'First we must pitch our tent,' said Orlando with his mouth full of tent pegs. 'Then we will have tea.'

The tent was soon up and Grace made the camp beds while her dear husband lit the stove; Pansy laid the tea-table.

Blanche dried herself and Tinkle licked the butter when nobody was looking.

Just as tea was over, the sky suddenly grew very dark

and the cats could hear thunder growling. Three heavy raindrops fell on their noses, Plip! Plop! Plup! Quickly they carried everything into the tent.

'Nobody must lean against or touch the inside of the tent,' said Orlando, 'because that will make the rain come right through.'

To keep the kittens happy until it was fine again, Orlando taught them how to play 'Cat's Cradle' with pieces of string.

Soon the storm was over and the first rainbow that the kittens

had ever seen appeared in their field and arched across the whole sky. They rushed out to catch it, but the further they ran, the further away seemed the rainbow.

They came back very cross and disappointed but cheered up when Orlando told them that was what rainbows always did, whether it was kittens or puppies who chased them.

It was now bedtime, and the stars and moon shone brightly. Orlando sprayed the inside of the tent with insecticide, to get rid of the gnats which had also crowded in to escape the rain; the kittens shut their eyes tightly to protect them from the spray.

The cats went to bed, but the kittens were so wide awake and excited at sleeping in a tent that Grace had to sing them a lullaby;

Orlando's tail gently beat time under his blanket. The purrs that came out of the tent quite scared the grasshopper, beetle and caterpillar, and even the old owl in the tree was rather alarmed.

Early next morning the sun shone, warming the grass and drying the dew so that the cats' paws needn't get wet. But the lazy creatures didn't wake up till quite late when an enormously loud voice bellowed 'MILK-O!' three times at the door of the tent. It was the Milk-maid with milk for their breakfast; a pail hung on one of her horns and a stool on the other. Orlando and Grace knew how to milk a cow and soon the pail was full.

After breakfast Orlando took Tinkle to the stream to teach him how to catch fish. He crouched on the bank and tickled the surface of the water with the tips of his whiskers; lots of sleepy little fish swam up from their beds to catch what they thought were delicious flies dancing on the stream, and tried to gobble them up.

But they weren't flies at all, only Orlando's whisker tips; he quickly and cleverly scooped some of the fish out of the water with his paws and took them home for Grace to fry.

When the cats had finished breakfast, they did the washing up and then set out on a day's walk, each with a rucksack filled with fish and egg sandwiches.

About mid-day they came to a mountain stream and Grace helped the kittens on with their bathing pants. They all dived in except little Tinkle who was frightened.

He rode on Orlando's back instead, and pretended to be a catfish; all cats can swim and soon he was as good at it as his sisters.

There were all sorts of interesting things in the water, some of which they ate, and they chased the water boatmen who hadn't had

such fun for a very long time.

Then the cats ate their sandwiches. After a rest, they climbed further up the mountain, which was steep and stony, with lots of striped and furry caterpillars. If the kittens hadn't already had such a good meal they might have eaten the caterpillars too, but more out of friendliness than hunger.

All at once they heard a sheep dog barking at them. Quickly hiding behind some stones they fluffed out their tails and hung them over the tops.

The dog could only see the cats' tails, and mistaking them for furry caterpillars, he went back to his sheep. The danger was over.

Purring happily they went on their way. It would have taken most people a whole day to climb that mountain, but the cats being such good climbers were at the top in a jiffy.

All the same, they were rather out of breath, so they lay down to rest. There was a glorious view of mountain tops and the sea with ships sailing upon it. Orlando took several photographs.

It was getting late and the sun went down. Tinkle, being tired, rode home in Orlando's rucksack. The next morning the Milk-maid awakened the cats again, and after breakfast Orlando said he must go to the Post Office and send Master a telegram to say they had arrived safely, and would he please forward any letters to them, at their present address. Grace stayed behind to tidy the tent and make the beds.

Orlando and the kittens went to ·the village. While Orlando wrote the telegram, the kittens chose picture postcards for all their friends.

When they had unstuck the stamps that would get on their whiskers, and fixed them on the postcards instead, they popped the cards in the letter-box and drove back to the camp.

The kittens spent the afternoon painting the view from the banks of the stream, and very good pictures they were. Pansy's was as nice upside down as right way up. Meanwhile, Grace prepared the supper.

'Tonight we'll have a sing-song round the camp fire,' said Orlando and the cats collected enough sticks to build a huge bon-fire. As soon as it was dark they lit it; you couldn't tell which were sparks and which were stars, the sky was so sprinkled with both.

Orlando played the banjo and Grace the harp, and the kittens joined in with trumpet and drum, concertina and cymbals. What lovely music they made! When it got late and the fire burnt low, they went to bed with their whiskers singed and smelling of wood smoke, but very happy.

Every day Orlando thought of something different to do. They played at acrobats among the tree tops. They drove to the sea in the

car, and picnicked in a ruined castle. One evening
they went to a fair and came home laden with all
the prizes they had won.

When their holiday was over, they 'struck' camp, which means to
pack it all up, and came home to Master. He measured the kittens
against the wall and marked their height with a pencil, to see how
much they had grown during their holiday.

'And now back to work,' purred Orlando as
he chased away all the impudent little mice
in the house.

Shirley Hughes

It's Too Frightening
For Me

ILLUSTRATED BY THE AUTHOR

Captain Grimthorpe's Visit

Jim and Arthur make friends with Mary, who lives with her Gran in an eerie old house by the railway footpath. One day Mary tells them that an unexpected visitor has arrived.

MARY put her head over the wall. She looked unhappy and had been crying.

She told them that the owner of the house, Captain Ginger Grimthorpe, had returned suddenly. He was very cross about the state of the place, and was threatening to send them away. Then they would be homeless! What was more, he did nothing but shout at them, and his dog kept barking at Uriah.

Now Jim and Arthur were never allowed to see Mary. She had very little chance to play anyway, as she had to spend so much time doing housework and helping Granny look after Captain

213

Grimthorpe. He was very demanding and sat about grumbling all day.

Poor Granny was quite worn out with all the work, and running up and down stairs.

But worse was to come.

Uriah had a big fight with Captain Grimthorpe's red-eyed dog.

He chased him all over the house and scratched him badly on the nose.

Captain Grimthorpe said that he wouldn't have that badly behaved cat about the place any longer, and he locked Uriah in an upstairs room.

He was to be sent away to a Cats' Home in the morning!

Jim and Arthur looked very grave when they heard this news. They liked Uriah very much, as he was such a jolly good fighter.

'Don't worry,' said Jim, 'we'll save him somehow.'

He was a very resourceful boy.

Together they thought of a plan. Mary was to get the key of the room in which Uriah was imprisoned. This was difficult, as it hung on a hook in the hall, just outside Captain Grimthorpe's sitting-room.

But Captain Grimthorpe always ate and drank too much at supper-time, and went off to sleep in a chair with his mouth open. The red-eyed dog did the same, stretched out on the rug.

Neither of them heard Mary as she slipped gently into the hall, took the key, and crept upstairs.

The plan was to put Uriah into a cat basket, and lower him out of the window on a long rope to the boys, who would be waiting in the yard below.

Uriah was very pleased to see Mary, and greeted her with loud purring. But he didn't like the look of the cat basket at all.

It was a terrible job to get him to go into it. At last the lid was safely tied down.

Leaning out, Mary could see Jim's and Arthur's upturned faces in the dark below the window. The basket wobbled on its rope as she started to lower it. Half-way down, Uriah decided he'd had enough.

He started to turn round and round inside, miaowing and scratching at the lid. The basket swung about wildly, banging against the sitting-room windowpane.

A light shone out. The window was thrown open, and Captain

Grimthorpe put his head out, peering into the darkness. At that moment Uriah's nose appeared under the lid of the basket.

In no time he had forced his way out and, clinging on for a moment with his claws, he made a great leap, landing right on top of Captain Grimthorpe's head!

There was a great uproar of wild cries and oaths, and a flurry of ginger curls. Uriah tore off into the night, wearing a ginger wig – and Captain Grimthorpe was quite bald!

Then a great many confusing things seemed to happen at once. They all crowded into the hall. Granny ran out of the kitchen, throwing her apron over her head and making a noise like a mad owl.

Bald Captain Grimthorpe stamped about, purple in the face with rage, calling for his wig. Mary was crying, 'Oh, Uriah, come back, come back!' And the red-eyed dog barked fiercely at everybody.

At this moment little Arthur stepped bravely forward, and said in a calm, clear voice: 'Captain Grimthorpe doesn't look a bit like his portrait up there without his hair on. I don't believe he's the same man at all!'

There was a sudden silence. Granny came out from under her apron and peered into Captain Grimthorpe's face.

'My goodness, I do believe the lad's right. You're not the same gentleman as I remember – I can see that now, even without my glasses.'

'His moustache doesn't look very real either,' observed Jim, 'it's sort of coming loose at one side.'

Captain Grimthorpe's face flushed to scarlet, and so did his shiny bald head. Muttering something under his breath, he retreated upstairs with his red-eyed dog at his heels.

'I always thought there was something funny about him,' said Mary. 'But don't let's bother about him now, the horrid old thing. We've *got* to find Uriah.'

For a long time they searched and called. It seemed hours before they heard an answering miaow, and Uriah came strolling up, shaking his back legs and pretending that nothing unusual had happened.

The next day Granny had some news for them. Captain Grimthorpe had disappeared! He had packed his things in the night and gone off with his dog, leaving nothing behind but a false moustache on the dressing-table.

Of course, he wasn't the real Captain Grimthorpe at all. It turned out that he was the Captain's lazy brother, Maurice, well known for his bad temper and dishonesty, who was going about in disguise to avoid paying his debts. Uriah had revealed his secret. Neither he nor his dog were ever seen again in those parts.

Kenneth Grahame

THE WIND
IN THE WILLOWS

ILLUSTRATED BY MIKE TERRY

THE FURTHER
ADVENTURES OF TOAD

*Toad has escaped from prison disguised as a washerwoman. Now he is
on his way back to Toad Hall, feeling very pleased with himself.*

TOAD got so puffed up with conceit that he made up a
song as he walked in praise of himself, and sang it at the
top of his voice, though there was no one to hear it but
him. It was perhaps the most conceited song that any animal ever
composed:

> The world has held great Heroes,
>   As history-books have showed;
> But never a name to go down to fame
>   Compared with that of Toad!

219

The clever men at Oxford
    Know all that there is to be knowed.
But they none of them know one half as much
    As intelligent Mr Toad!

The animals sat in the Ark and cried,
    Their tears in torrents flowed.
Who was it said, 'There's land ahead'?
    Encouraging Mr Toad!

The Army all saluted
    As they marched along the road.
Was it the King? Or Kitchener?
    No. It was Mr Toad.

The Queen and her Ladies-in-waiting
    Sat at the window and sewed.
She cried, 'Look! who's that *handsome* man?'
    They answered, 'Mr Toad.'

There was a great deal more of the same sort, but too dreadfully conceited to be written down. These are some of the milder verses.

He sang as he walked, and he walked as he sang, and got more inflated every minute. But his pride was shortly to have a severe fall.

After some miles of country lanes he reached the high road, and as he turned into it and glanced along its white length, he saw approaching him a speck that turned into a dot and then into a blob,

and then into something very familiar; and a double note of warning, only too well known, fell on his delighted ear.

'This is something like!' said the excited Toad. 'This is real life again, this is once more the great world from which I have been missed so long! I will hail them, my brothers of the wheel, and pitch them a yarn, of the sort that has been so successful hitherto; and they will give me a lift, of course, and then I will talk to them some more; and perhaps, with luck, it may even end in my driving up to Toad Hall in a motor-car! That will be one in the eye for Badger!'

He stepped confidently out into the road to hail the motor-car, which came along at an easy pace, slowing down as it neared the lane; when suddenly he became very pale, his heart turned to water, his knees shook and yielded under him, and he doubled up and collapsed with a sickening pain in his interior. And well he might, the unhappy animal; for the approaching car was the very one he had stolen out of the yard of the Red Lion Hotel on that fatal day when all his troubles began! And the people in it were the very same people he had sat and watched at luncheon in the coffee-room!

He sank down in a shabby, miserable heap in the road, murmuring to himself in his despair, 'It's all up! It's all over now! Chains and policemen again! Prison again! Dry bread and water again! O, what a fool I have been! What did I want to go strutting about the country for, singing conceited songs, and hailing people in broad day on the high road, instead of hiding till nightfall and slipping home quietly by back ways! O hapless Toad! O ill-fated animal!'

The terrible motor-car drew slowly nearer and nearer, till at last he heard it stop just short of him. Two gentlemen got out and walked round the trembling heap of crumpled misery lying in the road, and one of them said, 'O dear! This is very sad! Here is a poor old thing – a washerwoman apparently – who has fainted in the road! Perhaps she is overcome by the heat, poor creature; or possibly she has not had any food today. Let us lift her into the car and take her to the nearest village, where doubtless she has friends.'

They tenderly lifted Toad into the motor-car and propped him up with soft cushions, and proceeded on their way.

When Toad heard them talk in so kind and sympathetic a manner, he knew that he was not recognized, his courage began to revive, and he cautiously opened first one eye and then the other.

'Look!' said one of the gentlemen, 'she is better already. The fresh air is doing her good. How do you feel now, ma'am?'

'Thank you kindly, sir,' said Toad in a feeble voice, 'I'm feeling a great deal better!'

'That's right,' said the gentleman. 'Now keep quite still, and, above all, don't try to talk.'

'I won't,' said Toad. 'I was only thinking, if I might sit on the front seat there, beside the driver, where I could get the fresh air full in my face, I should soon be all right again.'

'What a very sensible woman!' said the gentleman. 'Of course you shall.' So they carefully helped Toad into the front seat beside the driver, and on they went once more.

Toad was almost himself again by now. He sat up, looked about him, and tried to beat down the tremors, the yearnings, the old cravings that rose up and beset him and took possession of him entirely.

'It is fate!' he said to himself. 'Why strive? Why struggle?' and he turned to the driver at his side.

'Please, sir,' he said, 'I wish you would kindly let me try and drive the car for a little. I've been watching you carefully, and it looks so easy and so interesting, and I should like to be able to tell my friends that once I had driven a motor-car!'

The driver laughed at the proposal, so heartily that the gentleman inquired what the matter was. When he heard, he said, to Toad's delight, 'Bravo, ma'am! I like your spirit. Let her have a try, and look after her. She won't do any harm.'

Toad eagerly scrambled into the seat vacated by the driver, took the steering-wheel in his hands, listened with affected

humility to the instructions given him, and set the car in motion, but very slowly and carefully at first, for he was determined to be prudent.

The gentlemen behind clapped their hands and applauded, and Toad heard them saying, 'How well she does it! Fancy a washerwoman driving a car as well as that, the first time!'

Toad went a little faster;

224

then faster still, and faster.

He heard the gentlemen call out warningly, 'Be careful, washerwoman!' And this annoyed him, and he began to lose his head.

The driver tried to interfere, but he pinned him down in his seat with one elbow, and put on full speed. The rush of air in his face, the hum of the engine, and the light jump of the car beneath him intoxicated his weak brain. 'Washerwoman, indeed!' he shouted recklessly. 'Ho, ho! I am the Toad, the motor-car snatcher, the prison-breaker, the Toad who always escapes! Sit still, and you shall know what driving really is, for you are in the hands of the famous, the skilful, the entirely fearless Toad!'

With a cry of horror the whole party rose and flung themselves on him. 'Seize him!' they cried. 'Seize the Toad, the wicked animal who stole our motor-car! Bind him, chain him, drag him to the nearest police-station! Down with the desperate and dangerous Toad!'

Alas! They should have thought, they ought to have been more prudent, they should have remembered to stop the motor-car somehow before playing any pranks of that sort. With a half-turn of the wheel the Toad sent the car crashing through the low hedge that ran along the roadside. One mighty bound, a violent shock, and the wheels of the car were churning up the thick mud of a horse-pond.

Toad found himself flying through the air with the strong upward rush and delicate curve of a swallow. He liked the motion, and was just beginning to wonder whether it would go on until he developed wings and turned into a Toad-bird, when he landed on his back with a thump, in the soft rich grass of a meadow. Sitting up, he could just see the motor-car in the pond, nearly submerged; the gentlemen and the driver, encumbered by their long coats, were floundering helplessly in the water.

He picked himself up rapidly and set off running across country as hard as he could, scrambling through hedges, jumping ditches, pounding across fields till he was breathless and weary, and had to settle down into an easy walk. When he had recovered his breath somewhat, and was able to think calmly, he began to giggle, and from giggling he took to laughing, and he laughed till he had to sit down under a hedge. 'Ho, ho!' he cried, in ecstasies of self-admiration. 'Toad again! Toad, as usual comes out on the top! Who was it got them to give him a lift? Who managed to get

on the front seat for the sake of fresh air? Who persuaded them into letting him see if he could drive? Who landed them all in a horse-pond? Who escaped, flying gaily and unscathed through the air, leaving the narrow-minded, grudging, timid excursionists in the mud where they should rightly be? Why, Toad, of course; clever Toad, great Toad, *good* Toad!'

Then he burst into song again, and chanted with uplifted voice:

> The motor-car went Poop-poop-poop,
>   As it raced along the road.
> Who was it steered it into a pond?
>   Ingenious Mr Toad!

'Oh, how clever I am! How clever, how clever, how very clev—'

A slight noise at a distance behind him made him turn his head and look. O horror! O misery! O despair!

About two fields off, a chauffeur in his leather gaiters and two large rural policemen were visible, running towards him as hard as they could go!

Poor Toad sprang to his feet and pelted away again, his heart in his mouth. 'O my!' he gasped, as he panted along, 'what an *ass* I am! What a *conceited* and heedless ass! Swaggering again! Shouting and singing songs again! Sitting still and gassing again! O my! O my! O my!'

He glanced back, and saw to his dismay that they were gaining on him. On he ran desperately, but kept looking back, and saw that they still gained steadily. He did his best, but he was a fat animal, and his legs were short, and still they gained. He could hear them close behind him now. Ceasing to heed where he was going, he struggled on blindly and wildly, looking back over his shoulder at the now triumphant enemy, when suddenly the earth failed under his feet, he grasped at the air, and, splash! he found himself head over ears in deep water, rapid water, water that bore him along with a force he could not contend with; and he knew that in his blind panic he had run straight into the river!

Janet and Allan Ahlberg

THE JACK POT

THERE was once a giant who had a problem with boys named Jack. Just because their name was Jack, these boys all thought it would be no problem to rob the giant, or slay him even (some of them were quite bloodthirsty), or otherwise make a nuisance of themselves in the house – pestering his wife, for instance. Each day the unhappy giant would find these little scamps hiding behind the milk bottles on the front step, or peeping out of his slippers in the sitting-room (not all of them were clever). Once he even found one trying to use the phone, for some reason. This was ridiculous, of course. He was too small to dial the number, let alone lift the receiver.

Well, the giant attempted to solve his problem in various ways. He put up notices saying: NO JACKS, JACKS KEEP OUT, and so on. Unfortunately, these boys were not much interested in reading, and anyway not all of them *could* read. They were all ages, you see. Some hadn't started school yet; one of them even crawled in!

The giant also tried 'Jack Powder' and bought a cat. But the powder didn't put them off, it only made them sneeze; and the cat preferred chasing birds to chasing boys. Besides, these particular boys often had little home-made swords with them. The giant tried other methods, but these didn't work either; and all the time the Jacks kept coming. What is worse, a few Jills (even) started showing up, and a Jock, too, as I recall.

231

Finally, when everything he could think of had failed, the giant came to a decision. Since he could not solve his problem, he would do his best to forget about it. With this in mind, he bought a large pot and put it in the kitchen next to the fridge. After that, whenever he or his wife or their small (fourteen-foot) son came upon a Jack, they would drop him into the pot and leave him there for a while. Each evening after tea the giant or his wife would stroll down the garden and empty the pot at the far end, which from the Jacks' point of view was about fifteen miles away.

Well, for a time this solution worked ... well. The giant recovered his peace of mind, and his wife cheered up, too. But something else also happened. You see, by and by the Jacks in the 'Jack Pot' got to know each other, became pals and, eventually, formed a football team, which has since made quite a name for itself in the local league. However, unfortunately (for the giant) they have not lost their interest in giants. And, of course, as you will probably have spotted, a Jack is one thing; a *team* of Jacks is something else.

Now the giant is plagued with Jacks, twelve at a time (eleven plus a substitute). Often they arrive roped together like climbers, and one way or another they are proving to be most ingenious. The giant is at his wits' end. His wife is threatening to leave him and go to her mother's. The cat has already run away.

So there it is: if you have any clever thoughts on this subject, there is one giant I know who would be glad to hear from you. His address is:

> Mr Biggs,
> Beanstalk House,
> The High Street.

> Perhaps you might drop him a line.
> (Not if your name is Jack, though.)

Charles Dickens

A CHRISTMAS CAROL

ILLUSTRATED BY QUENTIN BLAKE

MARLEY'S GHOST

Scrooge is a terrible old miser who has never given anything to anyone.
On Christmas night the ghost of his former business partner, Jacob Marley,
appears to him to utter an awful warning.

SCROOGE fell upon his knees, and clasped his hands before his face.

'Mercy!' he said. 'Dreadful apparition, why do you trouble me?'

'Man of the worldly mind!' replied the Ghost, 'do you believe in me or not?'

'I do,' said Scrooge. 'I must. But why do spirits walk the earth, and why do they come to me?'

'It is required of every man,' the Ghost returned, 'that the spirit within him should walk abroad among his fellow-men, and travel far and wide; and if that spirit goes not forth in life, it is condemned to do so after death. It is doomed to wander through the world – oh,

woe is me! – and witness what it cannot share, but might have shared on earth, and turned to happiness!'

Again the spectre raised a cry, and shook its chain and wrung its shadowy hands.

'You are fettered,' said Scrooge, trembling. 'Tell me why?'

'I wear the chain I forged in life,' replied the Ghost. 'I made it link by link, and yard by yard; I girded it on of my own free will, and of my own free will I wore it. Is its pattern strange to *you*?'

Scrooge trembled more and more.

'Or would you know,' pursued the Ghost, 'the weight and length of the strong coil you bear yourself? It was full as heavy and as long as this, seven Christmas Eves ago. You have laboured on it, since. It is a ponderous chain!'

Scrooge glanced about him on the floor, in the expectation of finding himself surrounded by some fifty or sixty fathoms of iron cable: but he could see nothing.

'Jacob,' he said, imploringly. 'Old Jacob Marley, tell me more. Speak comfort to me, Jacob.'

'I have none to give,' the Ghost replied. 'It comes from other regions, Ebenezer Scrooge, and is conveyed by other ministers, to other kinds of men. Nor can I tell you what I would. A very little more is all permitted to me. I cannot rest, I cannot stay, I cannot linger anywhere. My spirit never walked beyond our counting-house – mark me! – in life my spirit never roved beyond the narrow limits of our money-changing hole; and weary journeys lie before me!'

It was a habit with Scrooge, whenever he became thoughtful, to put his hands in his breeches' pockets. Pondering on what the Ghost had said, he did so now, but without lifting up his eyes, or getting off his knees.

'You must have been very slow about it, Jacob,' Scrooge observed, in a business-like manner, though with humility and deference.

'Slow!' the Ghost repeated.

'Seven years dead,' mused Scrooge. 'And travelling all the time?'

'The whole time,' said the Ghost. 'No rest, no peace. Incessant torture of remorse.'

'You travel fast?' said Scrooge.

'On the wings of the wind,' replied the Ghost.

'You might have got over a great quantity of ground in seven years,' said Scrooge.

The Ghost, on hearing this, set up another cry, and clanked its chain so hideously in the dead silence of the night, that the Ward would have been justified in indicting it for a nuisance.

'Oh! Captive, bound, and double-ironed,' cried the phantom, 'not to know, that ages of incessant labour by immortal creatures, for this earth must pass into eternity before the good of which it is susceptible is all developed. Not to know that any Christian spirit working kindly in its little sphere, whatever it may be, will find its mortal life too short for its vast means of usefulness. Not to know that no space of regret can make amends for one life's opportunity misused! Yet such was I! Oh! Such was I!'

'But you were always a good man of business, Jacob,' faltered Scrooge, who now began to apply this to himself.

'Business!' cried the Ghost, wringing its hands again. 'Mankind was my business. The common welfare was my business; charity, mercy, forbearance, and benevolence, were, all, my business. The dealings of my trade were but a drop of water in the comprehensive ocean of my business!'

It held up its chain at arm's length, as if that were the cause of all its unavailing grief, and flung it heavily upon the ground again.

'At this time of the rolling year,' the spectre said, 'I suffer most. Why did I walk through crowds of fellow-beings with my eyes turned down, and never raise them to that blessed Star which led the Wise Men to a poor abode? Were there no poor homes to which its light would have conducted *me*!'

Scrooge was very much dismayed to hear the spectre going on at this rate, and began to quake exceedingly.

'Hear me!' cried the Ghost. 'My time is nearly gone.'

'I will,' said Scrooge. 'But don't be hard upon me! Don't be flowery, Jacob! Pray!'

'How it is that I appear before you in a shape that you can see, I may not tell. I have sat invisible beside you many and many a day.'

It was not an agreeable idea. Scrooge shivered, and wiped the perspiration from his brow.

'That is no light part of my penance,' pursued the Ghost. 'I am here tonight to warn you, that you have yet a chance and hope of escaping my fate. A chance and hope of my procuring, Ebenezer.'

'You were always a good friend to me,' said Scrooge. 'Thank'ee!'

'You will be haunted,' resumed the Ghost, 'by Three Spirits.'

Scrooge's countenance fell almost as low as the Ghost's had done.

'Is that the chance and hope you mentioned, Jacob?' he demanded, in a faltering voice.

'It is.'

'I – I think I'd rather not,' said Scrooge.

'Without their visits,' said the Ghost, 'you cannot hope to shun the path I tread. Expect the first tomorrow, when the bell tolls one.'

'Couldn't I take 'em all at once, and have it over, Jacob?' hinted Scrooge.

'Expect the second on the next night at the same hour. The third upon the next night when the last stroke of twelve has ceased to vibrate. Look to see me no more; and look that, for your own sake, you remember what has passed between us!'

When it had said these words, the spectre took its wrapper from the table, and bound it round its head, as before. Scrooge knew this, by the smart sound its teeth made, when the jaws were brought together by the bandage. He ventured to raise his eyes again, and found his supernatural visitor confronting him in an erect attitude, with its chain wound over and about its arm.

The apparition walked backward from him; and at every step it took, the window raised itself a little, so that when the spectre reached it, it was wide open. It beckoned Scrooge to approach, which he did. When they were within two paces of each other, Marley's Ghost held up its hand, warning him to come no nearer. Scrooge stopped.

Not so much in obedience, as in surprise and fear: for on the raising of the hand, he became sensible of confused noises in the air; incoherent sounds of lamentation and regret; wailings inexpressibly sorrowful and self-accusatory. The spectre, after listening for a moment, joined in the mournful dirge; and floated out upon the bleak, dark night.

Scrooge followed to the window: desperate in his curiosity. He looked out.

The air filled with phantoms, wandering hither and thither, in restless haste, and moaning as they went. Every one of them wore chains like Marley's Ghost; some few (they might be guilty governments) were linked together; none were free. Many had been personally known to Scrooge in their lives. He had been quite familiar with one old ghost, in a white waistcoat, with a monstrous iron safe attached to its ankle, who cried piteously at being unable to assist a wretched woman with an infant, whom it saw below, upon a door-step. The misery with them all was, clearly, that they sought to interfere, for good, in human matters, and had lost the power for ever.

Whether these creatures faded into mist, or mist enshrouded them, he could not tell. But they and their spirit voices faded together; and the night became as it had been when he walked home.

Humphrey Carpenter

MR MAJEIKA AND THE GHOST HUNTER

ILLUSTRATED BY FRANK RODGERS

'NOW, everyone,' said Mr Potter, the head teacher of St Barty's School, at morning assembly, 'it's the school fête on Saturday, and I want you all to behave yourselves. Lady Debenham, the Chairman of the Governors, is coming to open it, and she gets very cross if children behave badly. I'm afraid that some of you have been pulling up the flowers in her garden as you come to school, and she's very angry about it. In fact she's talking about closing down St Barty's School, and sending you all to St James's School instead.'

There was a groan from everyone. St James's was a posh school in another part of the town, and no one wanted to be sent there. No one except Hamish Bigmore.

'I wish she *would* close rotten St Barty's,' said Hamish to Thomas and Peter, the twins, when they all got over to Class Three. 'Then we wouldn't have to be taught by Mr Majeika.'

Mr Majeika was Class Three's teacher. He was a wizard. He wasn't supposed to do magic, but sometimes he did, by mistake, or to stop Hamish Bigmore from being tiresome.

'I bet it was you who picked Lady Debenham's flowers,' said Jody, coming up to join the group.

'Of course it was,' grinned Hamish, who was limping a bit. 'The old so-and-so has put barbed wire round her garden, and I scratched myself getting in, but I pulled up her best daffodils. I'll do anything to close down this rubbishy old school.'

'This morning,' said Mr Majeika to Class Three, 'we're going to go on with this term's project, which as you know is wild flowers and plants. And today I'm going to tell you about herbal remedies.'

'What are they, Mr Majeika?' asked Thomas.

'It's what people used to use in the olden times before there were pills and medicines like we have today. When they were ill, or had hurt themselves, they made mixtures of herbs – things like lavender and mint and other leaves – as a cure. And it seems to have worked!'

'I've never heard such rubbish,' grumbled Hamish Bigmore. 'You can't cure anyone without X-rays and brain operations and blood transfusions and things like that. When *I* grow up, I'm going to be a famous surgeon.'

Mr Majeika smiled. 'Well, Hamish, you'd be surprised at what herbs could cure. In fact they still can. Am I right in thinking that you've got a bit of a scratch?'

Hamish glared at him. 'So what if I have?'

'Hm, yes,' said Mr Majeika, coming to look at it. 'A very nasty scratch . . . It looks as if it might have been made by barbed wire . . . Well, Hamish, I've got an old book of herbal remedies here, so let's see what we can do for you.'

Hamish protested, but in no time at all Mr Majeika had looked up some instructions in his book, and got the rest of Class Three to mix up herbs that they had been gathering on country walks during the term. Mr Majeika showed them how to make it into a sort of paste. Then he smeared the paste on Hamish's knee, and stood back to see what would happen.

What happened was that Hamish Bigmore vanished. Where he had been sitting there was an empty chair.

'Oh dear!' said Mr Majeika. 'I must have got the wrong remedy.'

'Has he turned into a frog again?' asked Jody, remembering what happened when Mr Majeika first came to St Barty's to teach Class Three.

'No, I haven't,' said Hamish's voice. 'I'm over here.' They all turned round, but they couldn't see anybody.

'Where?' said Peter.

'Here,' said Hamish's voice. And the waste-paper basket rose in the air, floated across the room, and emptied itself over Peter's head.

'Oh dear,' said Mr Majeika, examining his book of herbal remedies. 'I was on the wrong page. We've given Hamish a mixture that makes him invisible.'

Having an invisible Hamish ought to have been pleasant – 'After all,' said Thomas, 'he's an ugly brute, and it's nice not to be able to see him' – but really it was very tiresome. There was never five minutes' peace in Class Three. Anything wet, like paints or ink, kept floating into people's faces, and when you sat down your chair was pulled away so that you fell on the floor. And when Hamish got bored with tricks like that, he went around pulling people's hair and pinching them. Everyone kept trying to catch him, but it was no use, and Mr Majeika couldn't find a spell to make him visible again.

As the day of the fête got nearer, Hamish started making trouble in the other classes too.

'We're going to have an awful time on Saturday,' said Jody. 'I bet he's going to annoy Lady Debenham, so that she'll close the school.'

For answer, there came a cackle of laughter from the invisible Hamish.

'Ah, here she comes,' said Mr Potter. 'Dear Lady Debenham!' He bustled up to meet a very grand-looking woman in a hat.

'Couldn't help being late, Potter,' boomed Lady Debenham. 'Had to go to a meeting of the Society of Psychical Investigation.'

'Bicycles?' said Mr Potter vaguely. 'I didn't know you rode one.'

'No, no, man,' said Lady Debenham crossly, '*psychical*. It means ghosts. The Society exists to prove that ghosts are true, and we go around looking for them.'

'Ah yes,' said Mr Potter vaguely, leading Lady Debenham to where a small platform had been set up in the school playground. He went to the microphone and made a short speech of welcome.

Everyone clapped, and Lady Debenham boomed out: 'Thank you very much. Now, children, behave yourselves, or I shall have to think seriously about closing down St Barty's and sending you all to St James's. I declare this fête well and truly open.'

Everyone clapped again, and Jody brought a big bunch of flowers up to the platform. She was just going to present it to Lady

Debenham when something snatched it from her, and pushed it right in Lady Debenham's face.

'Oh no,' whispered Thomas, 'it's Hamish Bigmore.'

Mr Potter fussed around Lady Debenham, who was very angry, but after a few minutes she had calmed down a bit, and she began to go around the stalls with Mr Potter.

Her first call was at the Lucky Dip. She was just bending down to reach into the tub full of sawdust when her legs flew into the air and she landed face first in the tub.

'Hamish again!' whispered Jody. 'This is awful.'

It took a lot of time for Lady Debenham to get the sawdust out of her hair and clothes. By now she was in a furious temper. Mr Potter led her off to the home-made ice-cream stall.

'Oh dear,' whispered Jody, 'I can guess what's coming. Thomas and Pete, be quick! Run and get a sack, and let's see if we can't catch Hamish.'

They borrowed a sack from a pile set aside for the Sack Race, and ran over to the ice-cream stall. Already a large vanilla ice was hovering in the air over Lady Debenham's hat.

'Jump!' shouted Jody.

Thomas and Pete jumped, and brought the sack down over what they could feel was Hamish Bigmore. Unfortunately, they brought it down over Lady Debenham as well.

'It's all right,' said Mr Majeika to Jody, bustling up with a book under his arm. 'I've found the spell to stop him being invisible.'

'Too late!' said Jody, pointing to the ground. 'I'm afraid this is the end of St Barty's.'

On the ground, with the sack over her head, shouting at the top

of her voice, lay Lady Debenham. She was fighting the invisible Hamish Bigmore.

Mr Majeika, Jody, Thomas and Pete got the sack off her. To their amazement, she was smiling all over her face.

'We're so sorry,' said Thomas and Pete.

'Sorry?' beamed Lady Debenham. 'It was the greatest moment of my life! A real ghost! I couldn't see it, but I could hear it and feel it. My society will be delighted. And as for St Barty's, far from closing it down, I'm very, very proud of it. The only school in England with its own ghost.'

Jody looked at Thomas and Pete. 'Hamish Bigmore isn't going to like this one bit,' she grinned. 'He's saved St Barty's!'

Eleanor H. Porter

POLLYANNA

ILLUSTRATED BY PAUL HOWARD

THE LITTLE ATTIC ROOM

The orphaned Pollyanna comes to live with her strict maiden aunt.
Pollyanna's cheerful nature soon brightens up everybody's life, but first
she is given a very frosty welcome.

MISS Polly Harrington did not rise to meet her niece. She looked up from her book, it is true, as Nancy and the little girl appeared in the sitting-room doorway, and she held out a hand with 'duty' written large on every coldly extended finger.

'How do you do, Pollyanna? I —' She had no chance to say any more. Pollyanna had fairly flown across the room and flung herself into her aunt's scandalized, unyielding lap.

'Oh, Aunt Polly, Aunt Polly, I don't know how to be glad enough that you let me come to live with you,' she was sobbing. 'You don't know how perfectly lovely it is to have you and Nancy and all this after you've had just the Ladies' Aid!'

'Very likely – though I've not had the pleasure of the Ladies' Aid's acquaintance,' rejoined Miss Polly, stiffly, trying to unclasp the small, clinging fingers, and turning frowning eyes on Nancy in the doorway. 'Nancy, that will do. You may go. Pollyanna, be good enough, please, to stand erect in a proper manner. I don't know yet what you look like.'

Pollyanna drew back at once, laughing a little hysterically.

'No, I suppose you don't; but you see I'm not very much to look at, anyway, on account of the freckles. Oh, and I ought to explain about the red gingham and the black velvet basque with white spots on the elbows. I told Nancy how Father said –'

'Yes; well, never mind now what your father said,' interrupted Miss Polly crisply. 'You had a trunk, I presume?'

'Oh, yes, indeed, Aunt Polly. I've got a beautiful trunk that the Ladies' Aid gave me. I haven't got so very much in it – of my own, I mean. The barrels haven't had many clothes for little girls in them lately; but there were all Father's books, and Mrs White said she thought I ought to have those. You see, Father –'

'Pollyanna,' interrupted her aunt again sharply, 'there is one thing that might just as well be understood right away at once; and that is, I do not care to have you keep talking of your father to me.'

The little girl drew in her breath tremulously.

'Why, Aunt Polly, you – you – mean –' She hesitated, and her aunt filled the pause.

'We will go upstairs to your room. Your trunk is already there, I presume. I told Timothy to take it up – if you had one. You may follow me, Pollyanna.'

Without speaking Pollyanna turned and followed her aunt from

the room. Her eyes were brimming with tears, but her chin was bravely high.

'After all, I – I reckon I'm glad she doesn't want me to talk about Father,' Pollyanna was thinking. 'It'll be easier, maybe – if I don't talk about him. Probably, anyhow, that is why she told me not to talk about him.' And Pollyanna, convinced anew of her aunt's 'kindness', blinked off the tears and looked eagerly about her.

She was on the stairway now. Just ahead, her aunt's black silk skirt rustled luxuriously. Behind her an open door allowed a glimpse of soft-tinted rugs and satin-covered chairs. Beneath her feet a marvellous carpet was like green moss to the tread. On every side the gilt of picture-frames or the glint of sunlight through the filmy mesh of lace curtains flashed in her eyes.

'Oh, Aunt Polly, Aunt Polly,' breathed the little girl rapturously: 'what a perfectly lovely, lovely house! How awfully glad you must be you're so rich!'

'Poll*yanna*!' ejaculated her aunt, turning sharply about as she reached the head of the stairs. 'I'm surprised at you making a speech like that to me!'

'Why, Aunt Polly, *aren't* you?' queried Pollyanna, in frank wonder.

'Certainly not, Pollyanna. I hope I could not so far forget myself as to be sinfully proud of any gift the Lord has seen fit to bestow upon me,' declared the lady; 'certainly not of *riches*!'

Miss Polly turned and walked down the hall towards the attic stairway door. She was glad, now, that she had put the child in the attic room. Her idea at first had been to get her niece as far away as

possible from herself, and at the same time place her where her childish heedlessness would not destroy valuable furnishings. Now – with this evident strain of vanity showing thus early – it was all the more fortunate that the room planned for her was plain and sensible, thought Miss Polly.

Eagerly Pollyanna's small feet pattered behind her aunt. Still more eagerly her big blue eyes tried to look in all directions at once, that no thing of beauty or interest in this wonderful house might be passed unseen. Most eagerly of all her mind turned to the wondrously exciting problem about to be solved; behind which of these fascinating doors was waiting now her room – the dear, beautiful room, full of curtains, rugs, and pictures, that was to be her very own? Then, abruptly, her aunt opened a door and ascended another stairway.

There was little to be seen here. A bare wall rose on either side. At the top of the stairs wide reaches of shadowy space led to far corners where the roof came almost down to the floor, and where were stacked innumerable trunks and boxes. It was hot and stifling too. Unconsciously Pollyanna lifted her head higher – it seemed so hard to breathe. Then she saw that her aunt had thrown open a door at the right.

'There, Pollyanna, here is your room, and your trunk is here, I see. Have you your key?'

Pollyanna nodded dumbly. Her eyes were a little wide and frightened.

Her aunt frowned.

'When I ask a question, Pollyanna, I prefer that you should answer aloud – not merely with your head.'

'Yes, Aunt Polly.'

'Thank you; that is better. I believe you have everything that you need here,' she added, glancing at the well-filled towel-rack and water-pitcher. 'I will send Nancy up to help you unpack. Supper is at six o'clock,' she finished, as she left the room and swept downstairs.

For a moment after she had gone Pollyanna stood quite still, looking after her. Then she turned her wide eyes to the bare wall, the bare floor, the bare windows. She turned them last to the little trunk that had stood not so long before in her own little room in the far-away Western home. The next moment she stumbled blindly towards it and fell on her knees at its side covering her face with her hands.

Jill Murphy

THE WORST WITCH

ILLUSTRATED BY THE AUTHOR

THE PRESENTATION

Mildred Hubble doesn't exactly mean to break rules and annoy teachers, but things certainly happen when she is around. Miss Cackle's Academy for Witches will never be the same again. This extract begins with each young witch being given a witch's kitten.

THE presentation took place in the Great Hall, a huge stone room with rows of wooden benches, a raised platform at one end and shields and portraits all round the walls. The whole school had assembled, and Miss Cackle and Miss Hardbroom stood behind a table on the platform. On the table was a large wicker basket from which came mews and squeaks.

First of all everyone sang the school song, which went like this:

> Onward, ever striving onward,
> Proudly on our brooms we fly
> Straight and true above the treetops,
> Shadows on the moonlit sky.

Ne'er a day will pass before us
Wherr we have not tried our best,
Kept our cauldrons bubbling nicely,
Cast our spells and charms with zest.

Full of joy we mix our potions,
Working by each other's side.
When our days at school are over
Let us think of them with pride.

It was the usual type of school song, full of pride, joy and striving. Mildred had never yet mixed a potion with joy, nor flown her broomstick with pride – she was usually too busy trying to keep upright!

Anyway, when they had finished droning the last verse, Miss Cackle rang the little silver bell on her table and the girls marched up in single file to receive their kittens. Mildred was the last of all, and when she reached the table Miss Cackle pulled out of the basket not a sleek black kitten like all the others but a little tabby with white paws and the sort of fur that looked as if it had been out all night in a gale.

'We ran out of black ones,' explained Miss Cackle with a pleasant grin.

Miss Hardbroom smiled too, but nastily.

After the ceremony everyone rushed to see Mildred's kitten.

'I think H.B. had a hand in this somewhere,' said Maud darkly. ('H.B.' was their nickname for Miss Hardbroom.)

'I must admit, it does look a bit dim, doesn't it?' said Mildred, scratching the tabby kitten's head. 'But I don't really mind. I'll just have to think of another name — I was going to call it Sooty. Let's take them down to the playground and see what they make of broomstick riding.'

Almost all the first-year witches were in the yard trying to persuade their puzzled kittens to sit on their broomsticks. Several were already clinging on by their claws, and one kitten, belonging to a rather smug young witch named Ethel, was sitting bolt upright cleaning its paws, as if it had been broomstick riding all its life!

Riding a broomstick was no easy matter, as I have mentioned before. First, you ordered the stick to hover, and it hovered lengthways above the ground. Then you sat on it, gave it a sharp tap and away you flew. Once in the air you could make the stick do almost anything by saying, 'Right! Left! Stop! Down a bit!' and so on. The difficult part was balancing, for if you leaned a little too far to one side you could easily overbalance, in which case you would either fall off or find yourself hanging upside-down and then you would just have to hold on with your skirt over your head until a friend came to your rescue.

It had taken Mildred several weeks of falling off and crashing ore she could ride the broomstick reasonably well, and it looked as though her kitten was going to have the same trouble. When she put it on the end of the stick, it just fell off without even trying to hold on. After many attempts, Mildred picked up her kitten and gave it a shake.

'Listen!' she said severely. 'I think I shall have to call you Stupid. You don't even try to hold on. Everyone else is all right — look at all your friends.'

The kitten gazed at her sadly and licked her nose with its rough tongue.

'Oh, come on,' said Mildred, softening her voice. 'I'm not really angry with you. Let's try again.'

And she put the kitten back on the broomstick, from which it fell with a thud.

Maud was having better luck. Her kitten was hanging on grimly upside-down.

'Oh, well,' laughed Maud. 'It's a start.'

'Mine's useless,' said Mildred, sitting on the broomstick for a rest.

'Never mind,' Maud said. 'Think how hard it must be for them to hang on by their claws.'

An idea flashed into Mildred's head, and she dived into the school, leaving her kitten chasing a leaf along the ground and the broomstick still patiently hovering. She came out carrying her satchel which she hooked over the end of the broom and then bundled the kitten into it. The kitten's astounded face peeped out of the bag as Mildred flew delightedly round the yard.

'Look, Maud!' she called from ten feet up in the air.

'That's cheating!' said Maud, looking at the satchel.

Mildred flew back and landed on the ground laughing.

'I don't think H.B. will approve,' said Maud doubtfully.

'Quite right, Maud,' an icy voice behind them said. 'Mildred, my dear, possibly it would be even easier with handlebars and a saddle.'

Mildred blushed.

'I'm sorry, Miss Hardbroom,' she muttered. 'It doesn't balance very well – my kitten, so . . . I thought . . . perhaps . . .' Her voice trailed away under Miss Hardbroom's stony glare and Mildred unhooked her satchel and turned the bewildered kitten on to the ground.

'Girls!' Miss Hardbroom clapped her hands. 'I would remind you that there is a potion test tomorrow morning. That is all.'

So saying, she disappeared – literally.

'I wish she wouldn't do that,' whispered Maud, looking at the place where their form-mistress had been standing. 'You're never quite sure whether she's gone or not.'

'Right again, Maud,' came Miss Hardbroom's voice from nowhere.

Maud gulped and hurried back to her kitten.

Do you remember I told you about a certain young witch named Ethel who had succeeded in teaching her kitten from the very first try? Ethel was one of those lucky people for whom everything goes right. She was always top of the class, her spells always worked, and Miss Hardbroom never made any icy remarks to her. Because of this, Ethel was often rather bossy with the other girls.

On this occasion she had overheard the whole of Mildred's encounter with Miss Hardbroom and couldn't resist being nasty about it.

'I think Miss Cackle gave you that cat on purpose,' Ethel sneered. 'You're both as bad as each other.'

'Oh, be quiet,' said Mildred, trying to keep her temper. 'Anyway, it's not a bad cat. It'll learn in time.'

'Like you did?' Ethel went on. 'Wasn't it last week that you crashed into the dustbins?'

'*Look*, Ethel,' Mildred said, 'you'd better be quiet, because if you don't I shall . . .'

'Well?'

'I shall have to turn you into a frog – and I don't want to do that.'

Ethel gave a shriek of laughter.

'That's really funny!' she crowed. 'You don't even know the beginners' spells, let alone ones like that.'

Mildred blushed and looked very miserable.

'Go on, then!' cried Ethel. 'Go *on*, then, if you're so clever. *Turn* me into a frog! I'm waiting.'

It just so happened that Mildred did have an idea of that spell (she had been reading about it in the library). By now, everyone had crowded round, waiting to see what would happen, and Ethel was still jeering. It was unbearable.

Mildred muttered the spell under her breath – and Ethel vanished. In her place stood a small pink and grey pig.

Cries and shouts rent the air:

'Oh, no!'

'That's torn it!'

'You've done it now, Mildred!'

Mildred was horrified. 'Oh, Ethel,' she said. 'I'm sorry, but you did ask for it.'

The pig looked furious.

'You *beast*, Mildred Hubble!' it grunted. 'Change me back!'

At that moment Miss Hardbroom suddenly appeared in the middle of the yard.

'Where is Ethel Hallow?' she asked. 'Miss Bat would like to see her about extra chanting lessons.'

Her sharp gaze fell on the small pig which was grunting softly at her feet.

'What is this animal doing in the yard?' she asked, coldly.

Everyone looked at Mildred.

'I . . . let it in, Miss Hardbroom,' Mildred said hesitantly.

'Well, you can just let it out again, please,' said Miss Hardbroom.

'Oh, I can't do that!' gasped the unhappy Mildred. 'I mean, well . . . er . . . Couldn't I keep it as a pet?'

'I think you have quite enough trouble coping with yourself and that kitten without adding a pig to your worries,' replied Miss Hardbroom, staring at the tabby kitten which was peering round Mildred's ankles. 'Let it out at once! Now, where is Ethel?'

Mildred bent down.

'Ethel, dear,' she whispered coaxingly in the pig's ear. 'Will you please go out when I tell you to? Please, Ethel, I'll let you in again straight away afterwards.'

Pleading with people like Ethel never works. It only makes them feel their power.

'I *won't* go!' bellowed the pig. 'Miss Hardbroom, I *am* Ethel! Mildred Hubble turned me into a pig.'

Nothing ever surprised

Miss Hardbroom. Even this startling piece of news only caused her to raise one slanting eyebrow.

'Well, Mildred,' she said, 'I am glad to know that you have at least learned one thing since you came here. However, as you will have noticed in the Witches' Code, rule number seven, paragraph two, it is not customary to practise such tricks on your fellows. Please remove the spell at once.'

'I'm afraid I don't know how to,' Mildred confessed, in a very small voice.

Miss Hardbroom stared at her for a few moments.

'Then you had better go and look it up in the library,' she said, wearily. 'Take Ethel with you, and on your way drop in and tell Miss Bat why Ethel will be late.'

Mildred picked up her kitten and hurried inside, followed by the pig. Fortunately, Miss Bat was not in her room, but it was most embarrassing going into the library. Ethel was grunting loudly on purpose and everyone stared so much that Mildred could have crawled under the table.

'Hurry up,' moaned the pig.

'Oh, stop going on!' said Mildred, as she flicked hastily through the huge spell book. 'It's all your fault, anyway. You actually *asked* me to do it. I don't see why you're complaining.'

'I said a frog, not a pig,' said Ethel, pettily. 'You couldn't even do *that* right.'

Mildred ignored the grunting Ethel and kept looking in the book. It took her half an hour to find the right spell, and soon after that Ethel was her horrible self again. The people in the library were most surprised to see the pig suddenly change into a furious-looking Ethel.

'Now, don't be angry, Ethel,' Mildred said softly. 'Remember: "Silence in the library at all times".'

And she rushed into the corridor.

Frances Hodgson Burnett

THE SECRET GARDEN

ILLUSTRATED BY DIZ WALLIS

THE ROBIN WHO SHOWED THE WAY

When her parents die, Mary is sent from India to live in her uncle's rambling old house in Yorkshire. At first she hates her new home, but gradually she begins to fall under its spell. And then she finds a key.

THE skipping-rope was a wonderful thing. Mary counted and skipped, and skipped and counted, until her cheeks were quite red, and she was more interested than she had ever been since she was born. The sun was shining and a little wind was blowing – not a rough wind, but one which came in delightful little gusts and brought a fresh scent of newly turned earth with it. She skipped round the fountain garden, and up one walk and down another. She skipped at last into the kitchen-garden and saw Ben Weatherstaff digging and talking to his robin, which was hopping about him. She skipped down the walk towards him and he lifted his head and looked at her with a curious expression. She had wondered if he would notice her. She really wanted him to see her skip.

'Well!' he exclaimed. 'Upon my word! P'raps tha' art a young 'un, after all, an' p'raps tha's got child's blood in thy veins instead of sour buttermilk. Tha's skipped red into thy cheeks as sure as my name's Ben Weatherstaff. I wouldn't have believed tha' could do it.'

'I never skipped before,' Mary said. 'I'm just beginning. I can only go up to twenty.'

'Tha' keep on,' said Ben. 'Tha' shapes well enough at it for a young 'un that's lived with heathen. Just see how he's watchin' thee,' jerking his head towards the robin. 'He followed after thee yesterday. He'll be at it again today. He'll be bound to find out what th' skippin'-rope is. He's never seen one. Eh!' shaking his head at the bird, 'tha' curiosity will be th' death of thee some time if tha' doesn't look sharp.'

Mary skipped round all the gardens and round the orchard, resting every few minutes. At length she went to her own special walk and made up her mind to try if she could skip the whole length of it. It was a good long skip, and she began slowly, but before she had gone half-way down the path she was so hot and breathless that she was obliged to stop. She did not mind much, because she had already counted up to thirty. She stopped with a little laugh of

pleasure, and there, lo and behold, was the robin swaying on a long branch of ivy. He had followed her, and he greeted her with a chirp. As Mary had skipped towards him she felt something heavy in

270

her pocket strike against her at each jump, and when she saw the robin she laughed again.

'You showed me where the key was yesterday,' she said. 'You ought to show me the door today; but I don't believe you know!'

The robin flew from his swinging spray of ivy on to the top of the wall and he opened his beak and sang a loud, lovely trill, merely to show off. Nothing in the world is quite as adorably lovely as a robin when he shows off – and they are nearly always doing it.

Mary Lennox had heard a great deal about Magic in her Ayah's stories, and she always said what happened almost at that moment was Magic.

One of the nice little gusts of wind rushed down the walk, and it was a stronger one than the rest. It was strong enough to wave the branches of the trees, and it was more than strong enough to sway the trailing sprays of untrimmed ivy hanging from the wall. Mary had stepped close to the robin, and suddenly the gust of wind swung aside some loose ivy trails, and more suddenly still she jumped towards it and caught it in her hand. This she did because she had seen something under it – a round knob which had been covered by the leaves hanging over it. It was the knob of a door.

She put her hands under the leaves and began to pull and push them aside. Thick as the ivy hung, it nearly all was a loose and swinging curtain, though some had crept over wood and iron. Mary's heart began to thump and her hands to shake a little in her delight and excitement. The robin kept singing and twittering away and tilting his head on one side, as if he were as excited as she was. What was this under her hands which was square and made of iron and which her fingers found a hole in?

It was the lock of the door which had been closed ten years, and she put her hand in her pocket, drew out the key, and found it fitted the keyhole. She put the key in and turned it. It took two hands to do it, but it did turn.

And then she took a long breath and looked behind her up the long walk to see if anyone was coming. No one was coming. No one ever did come, it seemed, and she took another long breath, because she could not help it, and she held back the swinging curtain of ivy and pushed back the door which opened slowly – slowly.

Then she slipped through it, and shut it behind her, and stood with her back against it, looking about her and breathing quite fast with excitement, and wonder, and delight.

She was standing *inside* the secret garden.

It was the sweetest, most mysterious-looking place anyone could imagine. The high walls which shut it in were covered with the leafless stems of climbing roses, which were so thick that they were matted together. Mary Lennox knew they were roses because she had seen a great many roses in India. All the ground was covered with grass of a wintry brown, and out of it grew clumps of bushes which were surely rose-bushes if they were alive. There were numbers of standard roses which had so spread their branches that they were like little trees. There were other trees in the garden, and one of the things which made the place look strangest and loveliest was that climbing roses had run all over them and swung down long tendrils which made light swaying curtains, and here and there they had caught at each other or at a far-reaching branch and had crept from one tree to another and made lovely bridges of themselves. There were neither leaves nor roses on them now, and Mary did not know whether they were dead or alive, but their thin grey or brown branches and sprays looked like a sort of hazy mantle spreading over everything, walls, and trees, and even brown grass, where they had fallen from their fastenings and run along the ground. It was this hazy tangle from tree to tree which made it look so mysterious. Mary had thought it must be different from other gardens which had not been left all by themselves so long; and, indeed, it was different from any other place she had ever seen in her life.

'How still it is!' she whispered. 'How still!'

Then she waited a moment and listened at the stillness. The robin, who had flown to his tree-top, was still as all the rest. He did not even flutter his wings; he sat without stirring, and looked at Mary.

'No wonder it is still,' she whispered again. 'I am the first person who has spoken in here for ten years.'

Dodie Smith

THE ONE HUNDRED AND ONE DALMATIANS

ILLUSTRATED BY DAVID FRANKLAND

IN THE ENEMY'S CAMP

*Pongo and Missis are horrified when their puppies disappear,
particularly when they discover that Cruella de Vil is stealing
Dalmatian puppies in order to make herself a Dalmatian coat.
Pongo and Missis set off at once to rescue them.*

THE Colonel opened the gate to the stable yard. Missis gave a soft moan and hurled herself across the yard. She had seen Lucky. There he stood, at the back door, waiting for them. And behind him, in the long dark passage leading to the kitchen, were all his brothers and sisters. Who could describe what the mother and father felt during the next few minutes, as they tried to cuddle fifteen wagging, wriggling, licking puppies all at once? Everyone tried to be quiet but there were so many whimpers of bliss, so much happy snuffling, that the Sheepdog got nervous.

274

'Will they hear in there?' he asked
Lucky.

'What, the Badduns?' said Lucky –
rather indistinctly, because he had his
mother's ear in his mouth. 'No, they've
got their precious television on extra
loud.'

Still, the Colonel was relieved
when the first joy of the meeting was
over now.

'Quiet, now!' said Pongo.

'Quiet as mice!' said Missis.

But they were pleasantly surprised
at how quiet the pups instantly were.
The only sound came from some dead
leaves stirred by fifteen lashing little
tails.

'Now, still!' said Lucky.

All the tails stopped wagging.

'I'm teaching them to obey orders,'
said Lucky to the Colonel.

'Good boy, good boy. Let's see,
I made you a Corporal this afternoon, didn't I? I now make you a
Sergeant. If all goes well, you shall have your Commission next
week. Now I'm off to see my little pet, Tommy, have his bath.'

He told Pongo he would be back in a couple of hours. 'Slip out
and tell me what you think of things – or send the Sergeant with a
message.'

'Won't you come in and see the TV, sir?' said Lucky.

'Not while the Badduns are awake,' said the Colonel. 'Even *they* couldn't mistake me for a Dalmatian.'

As soon as he had gone, Lucky sent the other puppies to the kitchen, then took his father and mother in.

'You must stay at the back until your eyes get used to the dark,' he said.

And, indeed, it was dark! The only light came from the television screen and the kitchen fire, which were at opposite ends of the very large kitchen. And as the walls and ceiling were painted dark red, they reflected no light. It was extremely warm – much warmer than one fire could have made it. This was because there was central heating. Cruella de Vil had put it in when she planned to live in the house.

At last Pongo and Missis found they could see fairly well, and it was a strange sight they saw. Only a few feet away from the television, two men lay sprawled on old mattresses, their eyes fixed

on the screen. Behind them were ranged row after row of puppies, small pups at the front, large pups at the back. Those who did not care for television were asleep round the kitchen fire. The hot, red room was curiously cosy, though Pongo felt it was a bit like being inside a giant's mouth.

Lucky whispered: 'I thought we could settle Mother with the family and then I could show you round a bit. All the pups want to get a glimpse of you. Father, you are going to rescue them *all*?'

'I hope so,' said Pongo, earnestly – wondering more and more how he was going to manage it.

'I told them you would, but they've been pretty nervous. I'll just send the word round that they can count on you.' He whispered to a pup at the end of a row and the word travelled like wind over a cornfield. There was barely a sound that a human ear could have heard, except a couple of tail thumps, instantly repressed. All knew they must not give away the fact that Pongo was in their midst, and when he went silently along the rows there was scarcely a movement. But he could feel great waves of love and trust rolling towards him. And suddenly all the pups were real and living for him, not just a problem he had to face. He felt as if he were the father of them all. And he knew that he could never desert them.

He felt a special sympathy for the big pups in the two back rows. Some of them were fully half-grown – young dogs rather than puppies, lollopy creatures with clumsy feet. They made him remember his own, not very far away, youth. He wondered how long their skins would be safe from Cruella – would she have the patience to wait much longer? Did the big pups know that danger drew closer every day? Something in their eyes told him they did.

them had been in this horrible place for months, without hope until Lucky had spread the news that his father and mother were coming. Proud Lucky now, taking his father along the rows of hero-worshipping pups!

Blissfully happy, Missis sat with her children clustered about her. She had eyes only for them but they were determined she should not miss the television. She had never seen it before (Mr and Mrs Dearly did not care for it) and found it difficult to follow. The pups did not follow it completely as they had not yet learned enough human words; but they liked the little moving figures, and watched in the perpetual hope of seeing dogs on the screen.

'Can we have it when we get back home?' said the Cadpig.

'Indeed, you shall, my darling,' said Missis. Somehow, somehow, the Dearlys must be made to buy a set.

Pongo had now silently 'met' all the pups. He told Lucky he would like to have a good look at the Badduns. So Lucky took him a little way up the back staircase, where they could see without being noticed.

No one would have guessed that Saul and Jasper Baddun were brothers. Saul was heavy and dark, with a forehead so low that his bushy eyebrows often got tangled with his matted hair. Jasper was thin and fair, with a chin so sharp and pointed that it had worn holes in all his shirts – not that he had many. Both brothers looked very dirty.

'They never change their awful old clothes,' whispered Lucky, 'and they never wash. I don't think they are real humans, Father. Is there such a thing as a half-human?'

Pongo could well believe it after seeing the Badduns, but he

couldn't imagine what their non-human half was. It was no animal he had ever seen.

'Have they ill-treated any of you?' he asked, anxiously.

'No, they're too frightened of being bitten,' said Lucky. 'They're terrible cowards. Some of the big pups did think of attacking them – but there seemed no way of getting out. And if they'd killed the Badduns, there would have been no one to feed us. Oh, Father, how glad I am you've come!'

Pongo licked his son's ear. Pups, like boys, do not like fathers to be too sentimental (mothers are different), but this was a very private moment.

Then they went and sat with Missis and the family. It seemed strange that they could all be so peaceful right in the enemy's camp. Gradually the Pongos' puppies fell asleep – all except Lucky, Patch, and the Cadpig. Lucky was not sleepy. Patch was — but stayed awake because the Cadpig was awake. And the Cadpig stayed awake because she was crazy about television.

Many of the big pups, too, were lying down to sleep, stretching luxuriously, feeling — for the first time since they had been imprisoned in Hell Hall — that there was someone they could rely on. Pongo had come! And Missis, too. They had looked at her shyly, quite understanding that she must care for her own children first, but hoping she would have a little time for them later. Some of them could hardly remember their mothers. But the younger pups could remember theirs and they were not sleeping. Slowly, silently, they were inching their way towards Missis.

She had been watching the television, beginning to get the hang of it, with the Cadpig's help. Then some tiny sound, close at hand, brought her attention back to her family. But the sound had not come from her family. There were now nearly thirty puppies, not so very much bigger than her own, just a few feet away, all staring at her hopefully.

'Goodness, they're grubby,' was her first thought. 'Didn't their mothers teach them to wash themselves?'

Then she felt a pang of pity. What mother had any of them now? She smiled at them all — and they wrinkled their little noses in a return smile. Then she looked beyond them, to the larger pups. Some of the half-grown girls reminded her of herself at their age — so slim, so silly. They knew how to wash themselves but there were many things they didn't know, many ways in which they needed a mother's advice. And suddenly all the puppies were her puppies, she was their mother — just as Pongo had felt he was their father. And,

indeed, the younger ones creeping closer and closer to her were now so mingled with her own that she could scarcely tell where her little family ended and her larger family began.

Drowsiness spread throughout the warm, red room. Even the Baddun brothers dozed. They did not much like the programme that was on the television and wanted to be fresh for their very favourite programme, which was due later. Even Missis slept a little, knowing that Pongo would keep watch. At last only three pairs of eyes were open. Pongo was wide awake, thinking, thinking. Lucky was wide awake, for he thought of himself as a sentry, who must not sleep on duty. And the Cadpig was wide awake, watching her lovely, lovely television.

Suddenly there was a thunder of thumps on the front door. The sleeping pups awoke in alarm. The Baddun brothers lumbered to their feet and stumbled towards the door. But before they got there, it had been flung open.

Outside against the moonlit sky, stood a figure in a long white cloak.

It was Cruella de Vil.

Norman Hunter

Professor Branestawm's Christmas Tree

ILLUSTRATED BY CHRIS RIDDELL

Professor Branestawm's famous inventions
never turn out quite as planned.

THERE had never been a Christmas party at Professor Branestawm's house before. Because the Professor was always so immersed in thinking about new inventions he never had time to think about old customs. But this time the Professor was absolutely going to have a Christmas party, because he had invented a present-giving invention.

'I have always thought, Dedshott,' said the Professor to the Colonel,' that the – er – traditional Christmas tree offered possibilities for – um – development,' by which of course he meant it could be interestingly fiddled about with.

The Professor swung his new invention round, and the

Colonel got a daisy one on the ear from a sticking-out part of the machinery.

'My idea,' said the Professor, 'consists of a purely automatic Christmas tree, fitted with a mechanical present distributor coupled to a greetings-speaking device and a gift-wrapping attachment so that the − er − recipients receive their gifts suitably − um − ah − wrapped up and accompanied by a Christmas greeting.'

He pulled a lever, pressed some buttons and twiddled a twiddler.

'Pop, whizetty, chug, chug. *Good King Wenceslas*,' sang the machine.

'Look out!' cried the Professor. A highly decorative parcel shot out of the tree and landed on the Colonel's lap accompanied by a hearty 'Happy Christmas' from the tree and 'By Jove, what!' from the Colonel.

'Jolly clever, my word,' he grunted. 'How does it work, eh?'

The moment he asked the question, the Colonel wished he hadn't. He knew what would happen. The Professor would erupt in complicated explainings that would make his head go round and round. But this time it was all right. The Professor didn't explain anything. He came over all coy and said, 'Wait until my Christmas Party, Dedshott.'

The Professor's party started off all nice and ordinary, apart from the fact that it took place in November because the Professor couldn't wait to show off his invention. The guests arrived with presents for the Professor.

Mrs Flittersnoop gave him a sweet little rack with five hooks for his five pairs of spectacles, which was meant for keys, but anyway the

Professor hung his coat on it and collapsed the whole thing.

Colonel Dedshott weighed in with a paperweight made to look like a small cannon which made you feel you had to wait for it to go off though it never did.

The Mayor presented a photo of Pagwell High Street, in which he had a shop, in a green plush frame with gilt corners.

The Vicar handed the Professor a tastefully bound volume of his own sermons, autographed in mauve ink with ecclesiastical squiggles.

Sister Aggie's little girl was given a packet of toffee to give the Professor, but she ate it on the way and gave him instead a sticky kiss on the forehead, which helped to keep his spectacles on. The postman brought a collection of used stamps with something wrong with them which made them much more valuable than they ought to have been.

'Er – ah – thank you,' said the Professor. 'Now come this way please.' He led the way down the passage, and eventually after much pushing and excuse-me's they all got packed into his study where the automatic mechanical Christmas tree stood.

'Here is the present distributor,' said the Professor, pointing to a row of eager-looking levers. 'They are labelled with your names. All you have to – ah – do, is pull the lever with your name on.'

'Shall I declare the tree open?' said the Mayor and the Vicar, both at once. Then without waiting for an answer they both coughed and in very high-class voices said, 'I have pleasuah in declaring the tree open.'

Soon levers were being pulled, the machine was clanking away, the air was full of Christmas music and hearty greetings and the crash of paper parcels being excitably unwrapped.

The Mayor got a pair of silk stockings and a bottle of lavender water, which were really intended for Mrs Flittersnoop, because the Professor had got the names on the levers muddled up.

'Now that's what I call real kind,' cried Mrs Flittersnoop, then she said 'Oh!' in a rather pale voice when she found she'd got a packet of corn cure and a tin of tobacco shaped like a pillar box, which should have gone to the postman.

Sister Aggie found herself with a box of cigars. The Vicar had a china doll with no clothes on. Colonel Dedshott's present was a yellow bonnet with imitation cherries on it. The Pagwell Library man got a packet of large square dog biscuits and wondered if they were a new kind of book.

'I fear there has been some mistake,' murmured the Vicar. 'May I

be permitted to exchange this charming gift for something more suitable?' He pushed the china doll into the machine and pulled one of the levers. At the same time the Mayor and Sister Aggie pushed their presents back and started pressing not-meant-to-be-pressed buttons, to change their presents.

'No, no, no!' cried the Professor, clashing his spectacles.

But he was too late. The automatic Christmas tree evidently resented having its presents returned. It rang out a burst of Christmas bells that sounded like a fire engine, emitted a cloud of dirty green smoke, shouted 'Merry Christmas on the feast of Stephen,' and shot out of the house and down the road.

'After it!' roared the Colonel, who reckoned he knew how to deal with this situation.

They all tore after the machine that was shouting a mixed version of *The Twelve Days of Christmas*. Colonel Dedshott drew his sword and rushed at it. The machine took it away and returned it gift-wrapped.

'Five golden things,' sang the machine, careering down the road, giving out presents and Christmas wishes right and left. Three little boys with a November the Fifth Guy who were asking for pennies got instead a parcel of files and screwdrivers that were the Professor's Christmas present for himself. A lady coming out of a supermarket was presented with the Vicar's china doll and a yard and a half of *The Holly and the Ivy* sung out of tune.

'Dash round the other way and cut it off,' shouted the Colonel to the driver of a steamroller. But steamrollers are absolutely no good at dashing.

The Professor flew past on his bicycle in hot pursuit, but the machine scattered a box of coloured marbles on the road and he side-slipped into the Mayor's arms.

'Thirty-five maids a-dancing, ninety ladies singing, no end of a lot of swans splashing about, five gold rings,' sang the machine. It tore down Uppington Street, round the square, turned left into Wright Street, hotly pursued by the Professor, his guests and crowds

of Pagwell people who were shouting 'Stop, thief!' which was all they could think of to shout.

The machine ran out of presents and started picking up anything it could see and wrapping it in anything handy. A policeman held up his hand to make it stop and was given a piece of paving stone wrapped in an advertisement for second-hand bicycles.

On rushed the machine, across the High Street, smack into a smash–and–grab robber who was just dashing out of a jeweller's shop with a sack full of valuables.

'And a partridge up a gum tree,' shouted the machine. It sat on the robber, tore open the sack and was only just stopped from handing out watches and pearl necklaces all round by the arrival of an absolute heap of policemen. They arrested the robber and would have arrested the machine too, only Professor Branestawm arrived just in time to turn off the words and explain what had happened, which the policemen didn't believe anyway.

'Disturbing the peace, y'know,' said a police sergeant with three chins. 'Conduct likely to cause . . .'

But the Professor and the Colonel between them had got the Christmas tree apart, packed it into a passing wheelbarrow, given a new fifty-pence piece to the man who was pushing it and persuaded him to take it back to the Professor's house.

And everything turned out nicely because the jeweller gave the Professor a reward for catching the robber, so the Professor was able to buy some very handsome presents to give to everyone at Christmas, which he did by the very unoriginal but completely satisfactory method of handing them over and saying 'Happy um – ah – Christmas.'

Barbara Euphan Todd

WORZEL GUMMIDGE

ILLUSTRATED BY DAVID FRANKLAND

A VISITOR

Susan can't believe her ears when a tatty old scarecrow speaks to her.
But Worzel Gummidge is no ordinary scarecrow.

WHEN the farmer and his wife had left the kitchen, the
latch rattled again.

The tortoiseshell cat stopped washing her ears, and
glanced over her shoulder. Then the door opened very slowly and a
strange-looking visitor shambled
into the kitchen.

Susan recognized him almost at
once.

'Evenin'!' said the scarecrow, and
Susan wondered where she had
heard his voice before. He stared

round the room, then he coughed as sheep do on misty autumn
nights. Presently he said 'Evenin'!' again.

'Good evening!' said Susan politely.

'You needn't be scared,' he told her. 'It's only me!'

'I'm not scared. Only just at first, before I remembered, I thought
you might be a tramp.'

'Not me!' he replied. 'I'm a stand-still, that's what I am. I've been
standing still, rain and fine, day in and day out, roots down and roots
up.'

He began to walk crab-wise across the kitchen; one arm was
stretched out sideways, and the other one was crooked at the elbow.
As he walked, his bottle-straw boots made scratching noises on the
stone floor.

292

'You'll wonder what I've come for!' he said.

But Susan didn't particularly wonder, for it seemed perfectly natural for him to be there. She stared at him, and decided that his straw boots could not be really comfortable for walking in.

'I've come to save you a journey,' said the scarecrow. 'At least, partly to save you a journey and partly to save myself from missing it.'

'From missing what?' asked Susan.

'The umbrella. Where is it?'

Susan was so astonished that she could only point to the row of pegs on the door. The farmer's coat hung on one, and Mrs Braithewaite's overall was on another. The third peg held a cap and the scarecrow's umbrella, or what was left of it.

293

'I'm so sorry,' said Susan at last, 'but you didn't seem to be using it, and so –'

'I know all about that,' replied the scarecrow. 'I heard you argufying.'

'If we'd known you could talk, we'd have asked you to lend us the umbrella,' explained Susan. 'I did think though that I heard you speak, just as we were going away.'

'That's right. But I'm not much of a talker except now and again.'

The scarecrow took his umbrella down from the peg, and stroked it once or twice. Then he dropped it with a clatter.

'I might as well sit down,' he said, and moved towards the fireplace. 'How do you?'

'Very well, thank you,' said Susan politely, though she couldn't think why he was asking the question then.

The scarecrow looked puzzled. 'I mean,' he explained, 'I mean how do I sit? Is it difficult the first time you do it?'

But Susan couldn't remember, for she was so very used to sitting. She continued to look at the scarecrow. His face certainly was remarkably like a turnip, and yet his widely grinning mouth had a kindly expression. As he waited, the lump in the middle of his face began to look quite like a real nose. Just as Susan was wondering what to say next, he lifted the little hen robin from his pocket, and gently rubbed his cheek with her wing feathers. 'It's still a bit damp outside,' he explained, as he popped the bird back into its place. 'I always use her as a handkychiff.'

Then he suddenly moved backwards, lifted both feet together and sat down on the hearthrug with his feet sticking straight out in front of him.

'So that's how they sit,' thought Susan.

The tortoiseshell cat looked very offended, and stalked out into the scullery.

The robin fluttered back into his pocket and began to make rustling noises inside it. Susan remembered then that the scarecrow in Ten-acre field had had a robin's nest in its breast pocket. Just as she was wondering if there was a father robin, another little bird suddenly hopped out from his hiding-place under the scarecrow's wide-brimmed hat, looked round importantly, straddled his legs, jerked his tail. Then, encouraged by the reflection of the fire gleaming on the sunny surface of a warming-pan, he began a mad little song.

Susan leaned forward and touched the scarecrow on the knee. She longed to be friendly with anybody who kept robins in a coat pocket.

'What's your name?' she asked.

'Gummidge,' he replied. 'I'm Worzel Gummidge. I chose the name this morning. My granfer's name was Bogle.'

'Gummidge isn't a very pretty name,' objected Susan.

'No,' he replied. 'It's as ugly as I am.'

Susan looked at him. His hat was awry over his turnipy face. A shabby black coat hung from his shoulders, and one arm was still akimbo. But she noticed that he had managed to bend his knees a little, and that his fingers, which two minutes before had looked like bits of stick, were more human now; they even showed lumps that might possibly be mistaken for knuckles. He was growing less like a scarecrow every minute. Soon, thought Susan, he might look more like a man than Farmer Braithewaite.

'Gummidge isn't pretty,' she said, 'but it's a very interesting name.'

'Ooh aye!' he agreed. 'But then, I've a power of things to interest me — roots tickling and shooting, rooks lifting in the wind, rabbits here, there, and scattered in a minute. Give over now, do!' This last remark was made to the cock-robin, who was pecking at his greenly-bearded chin.

'How old are you?' asked Susan.

'All manner of ages,' replied the scarecrow. 'My face is one age, and my feet are another, and my arms are the oldest of all.'

'How very, very queer,' said Susan.

''Tis usual with scarecrows,' replied Gummidge. 'And it's a good way too. I get a lot of birthdays, one for my face and another for my middle and another for my hands, and so on.'

'But do you get presents?'

'Well, I haven't had many so far,' confessed Gummidge, 'but then I've seldom thought about having birthdays. *Will* you give over!' He raised a hand and pushed the little bird back again under the shadow of his hat.

'Do you often walk about?' asked Susan.

'Never done it before!' declared Gummidge. 'But I says to myself

last night, when I was standing in Ten-acre field, I says to myself, "You ought to go about the world and see things, same as the rabbits do. What's the use of having smart legs," I said, "if you don't use them!"' Gummidge stroked his shabby trousers proudly. 'I says to myself, "You might as well be rooted for all the travelling you do." So this evening after the rooks had stopped acting silly, I pulled up my feet and walked about a bit. Then I went up to the sheep pens and had a bit of a talk with one of the ewes.'

'Which one?' asked Susan.

'Eliza, her that has the black face,' replied Gummidge. 'But she was a bit short with me; she was so taken up with her son and daughter.'

'Has she got lambs?' asked Susan.

'Ooh aye! She's got a black son and a white daughter. She says they're the finest lambs in Scatterbrook and that they're wearing the best tails *she's* ever seen. I said to her, I said, "You needn't talk; there's a hazel bush at the corner of Ten-acre which is fair covered with lambs' tails, and she doesn't make such a song about it." After that the ewe turned her back on me.'

'Why did you come here?' asked Susan.

'Well, I had thought about going to London instead,' replied the scarecrow. 'I thought I'd go to London, till I met a mouse in the lane and she changed my mind for me.'

'Why did she?'

'She had been to London herself. She was a field-mouse, and she'd heard tell of stowaways. So she stowed herself away in a market basket and she saw Piccadilly.'

'Did she like it?' asked Susan.

'Well, I don't know about that,' replied Gummidge. 'But she saw a policeman, and he was dressed just the same as the one in Scatterbrook, and she said if they couldn't do better than that in Piccadilly, she'd come home again. And she said they told such lies. There's a place they call St-Martin-in-the-Fields, and it isn't in the fields at all. There's another place called Shepherd's Market, and she said there wasn't a shepherd there. So she said London was all a sham and that it was trying to copy Scatterbrook, so she came home again. And I've come here to fetch my umbrella.'

'Are you going to stay in Scatterbrook?' asked Susan eagerly. She had taken a fancy to Worzel Gummidge and she hoped that he'd teach her how to talk to sheep and how to tame robins.

'I might,' said Gummidge carelessly. He raised a hand and lifted a piece of mud from the place where his right ear should have been. Susan saw that his fingers moved stiffly as scissors and that his thumbs were like sticks. Then his head drooped forward and he fell asleep.

The Brothers Grimm

THE FROG PRINCE

RETOLD BY WENDY COOLING
ILLUSTRATED BY TONY ROSS

LONG, long ago when the world was full of magic and wonder, and wishes came true, there lived a beautiful Princess. She lived in a splendid palace with her father, a wise and honest King, and her older sisters. The youngest Princess was so beautiful that anyone who saw her smiled and so the royal palace was a very happy place.

In the summertime the youngest Princess loved to walk out of the palace to play in the woods where it was cool and pleasant. Best of all she loved playing with her favourite toy – a glittering ball made out of real gold. Often she would stop and rest by an ancient, very deep well and gaze into the still water.

One day as the Princess wandered through the woods she was playing her usual game of throwing and catching. She was good at this game and was shocked when she missed the ball and saw it roll away and fall into the well. She heard the loud, echoing splash as it hit the dark water and was sure that her golden ball was lost for ever.

Favourite toys are very important things and the beautiful

Princess was very sad to lose hers, so sad that she sighed softly and a few tears rolled down her cheeks. She couldn't bear to think that she would never play with her ball again and she covered her face as she cried. Her grief was interrupted by a voice saying, 'Please don't cry. You're too beautiful to be sad. Tell me what is troubling you.'

The Princess uncovered her eyes and was amazed to find herself looking into the huge eyes of an ugly green frog. 'Oh!' she cried. 'My favourite ball has rolled into the well and I shall never see it again. I would give anything to get it back.'

The frog seemed to look right through her eyes and into her head as he asked, 'Anything? Would you really give *anything* to get your lost ball back?'

'Yes!' cried the Princess. 'My golden crown, my jewels, my clothes – anything I have.'

'Your jewels and your clothes are no good to me,' said the frog, 'but I will dive into the well and find your ball if you will make me a promise. Will you promise to let me return with you to the palace, let me live with you, let me eat from your golden plate, let me sleep in your bed and let me make you my wife?'

The Princess thought the idea of marrying the horrid, slimy frog was just too silly to be taken seriously. But she did want her golden ball back, so, although she was laughing inside, she agreed to all the frog asked. She watched as he closed his large eyes, stretched his long back legs and dived, straight as an arrow into the well.

The frog returned to the surface faster than you can imagine, carrying the Princess's ball in his mouth. As soon as he dropped the ball the Princess picked it up and ran home as fast as she could.

Behind her she could hear the frog's croaky voice calling, 'Wait for me, wait for me! I can't run as quickly as you, please wait for me.' But his voice became quieter and quieter as the Princess sped on to the palace. She sighed with relief as she vanished inside and closed the door behind her, quite certain that she would never see the frog again.

Next day the Princess was sitting down to dinner with her family when there was a strange slipping noise outside, followed by a soft knocking at the door and a voice almost singing:

'Let me in, dear Princess,
Open the door, let me in.

Remember your promise,
Let me in, let me in.'

The Princess ran to the door and was horrified to see the frog
waiting in the hall. Angrily she slammed the door and went back to
the table.

'Who was that?' asked the King. 'Why are you so angry?'

'Ugh!' said the Princess, shivering with disgust. 'It was a nasty
old frog. He found my golden ball for me after it had fallen into the
well and he made me make a stupid promise to let him come to the
palace and live with me, sharing my food and my bed.'

The King frowned. 'If you make a promise you must keep it,' he
said sternly. 'Let the frog come in.'

The Princess loved her father and always did as he said, so she
reluctantly opened the door. But she shuddered as the frog hopped
into the room and up to her chair.

'Lift me up, dear Princess. Let me eat from your golden plate
and drink from your golden cup,' said the frog.

The Princess saw the stern look on her father's face and forced
herself to do as she had been asked. She was so upset to see the frog
at the table that she ate nothing at all, but the frog enjoyed the best
meal he had eaten for a very long time.

At last the frog said, 'Princess, I am tired after my long journey
to the palace. Please carry me up to your bed so that I can rest for
the night.'

The Princess knew now that she was bound by her promise, so,
with an ill grace, she carried the frog up to her bed and lay down
beside him, scarcely daring to move in case she touched him.

'Now,' said the frog, 'you must kiss me goodnight before we go to sleep.'

The Princess was filled with horror. How could she bring herself to kiss an ugly, slimy frog? But she could almost hear the voice of her father saying, 'A promise is a promise,' so she moved slowly towards the frog, closed her eyes and waited for the kiss.

Well, what a surprise! The frog's kiss was not the nasty wet kiss that she had feared, but a soft, gentle kiss that she rather enjoyed.

The Princess opened her eyes and there beside her was, not the frog she disliked so much, but a smiling, handsome Prince!

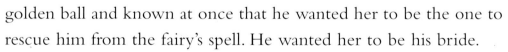

The Prince told the Princess of his long enchantment by a wicked fairy, an enchant- ment that could only be lifted by a beautiful Princess. He told her how he had seen her playing with the golden ball and known at once that he wanted her to be the one to rescue him from the fairy's spell. He wanted her to be his bride.

The wedding of the Prince and Princess was the most beautiful you can imagine: a day of flowers, silks, satins, smiles and happiness, and all the people joined in the great celebrations. The bride and groom then rode away in a golden carriage pulled by six white horses, to the Prince's kingdom where they lived happily ever after.

∾

INDEX OF AUTHORS

ACKNOWLEDGEMENTS

∾

*The editor and publishers gratefully acknowledge the following
for permission to reproduce copyright stories in this book:*

'The Jack Pot' by Janet and Allan Ahlberg from *The Clothes Horse and Other Stories*, first published by Viking Kestrel 1987, copyright © Janet and Allan Ahlberg, 1987, text and illustrations reprinted by kind permission of the author; 'Humblepuppy' by Joan Aiken from *A Harp of Fishbones*, published by Jonathan Cape, copyright © Joan Aiken Enterprises Ltd, 1972 UK, copyright © Joan Aiken, 1971 US, reprinted by permission of A. M. Heath & Company Limited and Brandt & Brandt Literary Agents Inc., New York; 'Mr Majeika and the Ghost Hunter' by Humphrey Carpenter, first published in Puffin Flight 1988, copyright © Humphrey Carpenter, 1988, reprinted by kind permission of the author c/o Cecily Ware Literary Agents; 'The Emperor's New Clothes' and 'The Frog Prince' retold by Wendy Cooling, copyright © Wendy Cooling, 1996; 'Adding up to Zero' by Helen Cresswell, copyright © Helen Cresswell, reprinted by permission of A. M. Heath & Company Limited; 'Spotty Powder' by Roald Dahl first appeared in *Puffin Post* Vol. 7 No. 1 1973, copyright © Roald Dahl Nominee Ltd, 1973, reprinted by kind permission of the executors of the Estate of Roald Dahl; 'A Christmas Carol' by Charles Dickens, illustrated by Quentin Blake, published by Pavilion Books 1995, copyright © Quentin Blake 1995, reprinted by permission of Pavilion Books and Margaret McElderry Books, a division of Simon & Schuster Children's Books; 'The Further Adventures of Toad' by Kenneth Grahame from *The Wind in the Willows*, published by Methuen 1908, copyright © The University Chest, 1908, reprinted by permission of Curtis Brown Ltd, London; 'Orlando the Marmalade Cat: A Camping Holiday' by Kathleen Hale, published in Country Life 1938, copyright © Kathleen Hale, 1938, reprinted by permission of Frederick Warne & Co.; *It's Too Frightening for Me* by Shirley Hughes, published by Hodder & Stoughton 1977, copyright © Shirley Hughes, 1977, reprinted by kind permission of the author; 'Professor Branestawm's Christmas Tree' by Norman Hunter from *The Peculiar Triumph of Professor Branestawm*, published by The Bodley Head 1970, copyright © The Estate of Norman Hunter, 1970, reprinted by permission of The Bodley Head, Random House UK Limited; 'How the Camel Got His Hump' by Rudyard Kipling from *Just So Stories*, published by Macmillan 1902, copyright © The National Trust for Places of Historic Interest and Natural Beauty, 1902, reprinted by permission of A. P. Watt Ltd on behalf of The National Trust for Places of Historic Interest and Natural Beauty; 'The Magic Crossing' by Dick King-Smith from *The Hodgeheg*, published by Hamish Hamilton Ltd 1987, copyright © Dick King-Smith, 1987, reprinted by kind permission of the author c/o A. P. Watt Ltd; 'Edmund and The Wardrobe' by C. S. Lewis from *The Lion, the Witch and the Wardrobe*, first published by Geoffrey Bles 1950, copyright © The Estate of C. S. Lewis, 1950, reprinted by permission of HarperCollins Publishers Limited; 'The Runaway Reptiles' by Margaret Mahy from *Bubble Trouble and Other Poems and Stories*, published by Hamish Hamilton Ltd 1991, copyright © Margaret Mahy, 1991, reprinted by permission of Penguin Books Ltd; 'Pooh and Piglet Go Hunting and Nearly Catch a Woozle' by A. A. Milne from *Winnie-the-Pooh*, published by Methuen Children's Books 1926, copyright © A. A. Milne, 1926, reprinted by permission of Reed Books and Dutton Children's Books US, illustrations by E. H. Shepard copyright under the Berne Conventions and in the USA copyright © 1926 by E. P. Dutton, copyright renewal 1954 by A. A. Milne, colouring copyright © Dutton Children's Books, 1991, reprinted